WINE COUNTRY COURIER

Community Buzz

The Napa Valley Has Two More Ashtons to Contend With

As if we didn't have enough, what with the two factions of the same family running two rival vineyards! But these Ashtons—Grant Ashton and his niece Abigail—don't carry the heady aromas of fine wines, but the questionable aromas of hay and horses!

Case in point, Dr. Abigail Ashton, traveling all the way from Nebraska with her veterinary degree in hand, comes to beautiful Napa and spends most of her time in the Louret Vineyard's stable!

Although considering that hunky Louret harvest master and part-time rodeo stud Russ Gannon spends most of his free time in the Louret stables, as well, perhaps I don't blame the poor girl. After all, if there is any reason at all to spend time in a stinky stable, rolling in the hay with a stud like Gannon would be it!

Dear Reader,

It's Valentine's Day, time for an evening to remember. Perhaps your perfect night consists of candlelight and a special meal, or a walk along a deserted beach in the moonlight, or a wonderful cuddle beside a fire. My fantasy of what the perfect night entails includes 1) a *very* sexy television actor who starred in a recently canceled WB series 2) a dark, quiet corner in an elegant restaurant 3) a conversation that ends with a daring proposition to… Sorry, some things a girl just has to keep a secret! Whatever your evening to remember entails, here's hoping it's unforgettable.

This month in Silhouette Desire, we also offer you *reads* to remember long into the evening. Kathie DeNosky's *A Rare Sensation* is the second title in DYNASTIES: THE ASHTONS, our compelling continuity set in Napa Valley. Dixie Browning continues her fabulous DIVAS WHO DISH miniseries with *Her Man Upstairs*.

We also have the wonderful Emilie Rose whose *Breathless Passion* will leave you…breathless. In *Out of Uniform*, Amy J. Fetzer presents a wonderful military hero you'll be dreaming about. Margaret Allison is back with an alpha male who has *A Single Demand* for this Cinderella heroine. And welcome Heidi Betts to the Desire lineup with her scintillating surrogacy story, *Bought by a Millionaire*.

Here's to a memorable Valentine's Day…however you choose to enjoy it!

Happy reading,

Melissa Jeglinski

Melissa Jeglinski
Senior Editor
Silhouette Books

Please address questions and book requests to:
Silhouette Reader Service
U.S.: 3010 Walden Ave., P.O. Box 1325, Buffalo, NY 14269
Canadian: P.O. Box 609, Fort Erie, Ont. L2A 5X3

DYNASTIES: THE ASHTONS

A RARE SENSATION

Kathie DeNosky

Published by Silhouette Books
America's Publisher of Contemporary Romance

Special thanks and acknowledgment are given
to Kathie DeNosky for her contribution to the
DYNASTIES: THE ASHTONS series.

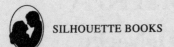 SILHOUETTE BOOKS

ISBN 0-373-76633-5

A RARE SENSATION

Visit Silhouette Books at www.eHarlequin.com

Printed in U.S.A.

Books by Kathie DeNosky

Silhouette Desire

Did You Say Married?! #1296
The Rough And Ready Rancher #1355
His Baby Surprise #1374
Maternally Yours #1418
Cassie's Cowboy Daddy #1439
Cowboy Boss #1457
A Lawman in Her Stocking #1475
In Bed with the Enemy #1521
Lonetree Ranchers: Brant #1521
Lonetree Ranchers: Morgan #1540
Lonetree Ranchers: Colt #1551
Remembering One Wild Night #1559
Baby at His Convenience #1595
A Rare Sensation #1633

Silhouette Books

Home for the Holidays
"New Year's Baby"

KATHIE DeNOSKY

lives in her native southern Illinois with her husband and
one very spoiled Jack Russell terrier. She writes highly
sensual stories with a generous amount of humor.
Kathie's books have appeared on the Waldenbooks best-
seller list and received the Write Touch Readers' Award
from WisRWA and the National Readers' Choice Award.
She enjoys going to rodeos, traveling to research settings
for her books and listening to country music. Readers
may contact Kathie at: P.O. Box 2064, Herrin, Illinois
62948-5264 or e-mail her at kathie@kathiedenosky.com.

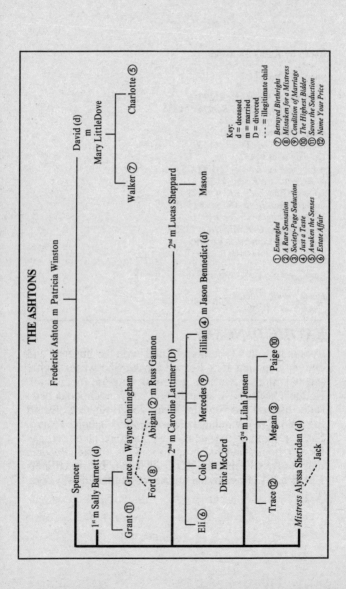

THE ASHTONS

Frederick Ashton m Patricia Winston

David (d)
m
Mary LittleDove

Walker ⑦   Charlotte ⑤

Mason

Spencer
Grace m Wayne Cunningham
Abigail ② m Russ Gannon
Ford ⑧

2ⁿd m Lucas Sheppard

Jillian ④ m Jason Bennedict (d)

1ˢᵗ m Sally Barnett (d)

Grant ⑪

2ⁿd m Caroline Lattimer (D)

Mercedes ⑨

Cole ①
m
Dixie McCord

3ʳd m Liiah Jensen

Eli ⑥

Megan ③   Paige ⑩

Trace ⑫

Mistress Alyssa Sheridan (d)

Jack

Key:
d = deceased
m = married
D = divorced
- - - = illegitimate child

① *Entangled*
② *A Rare Sensation*
③ *Society-Page Seduction*
④ *Just a Taste*
⑤ *Awaken the Senses*
⑥ *Estate Affair*
⑦ *Betrayed Birthright*
⑧ *Mistaken for a Mistress*
⑨ *Condition of Marriage*
⑩ *The Highest Bidder*
⑪ *Savor the Seduction*
⑫ *Name Your Price*

Prologue

1963

Spencer Ashton glanced over at his wife, Sally, and the two squalling babies on her lap as he drove away from the Crawley cemetery. Damn, but he looked forward to not having to suffer any more of Sally's pathetic adoration, or listen to the twins' constant howling. Grant wasn't so bad. At least the boy shut up once in a while. But Grace's nonstop screeching made life a living hell. And one that Spencer had every intention of escaping.

He glanced in the truck's rearview mirror at the cemetery workers filling in the new grave. Now that his controlling old man was dead of a heart attack, Spencer was free. Free to be rid of Sally and the twins. Free to shake the dust off his heels and pursue his own dreams. Free to leave Crawley, Nebraska, as far behind as his old Ford and the hundred bucks in his pocket would take him.

"Can't you shut that kid up?" he growled when the baby girl's screaming reached a crescendo.

"She's teething," Sally said, in that singsong voice that made his skin crawl. She kissed the top of the kid's little, bald head. "There, there, Gracie. Daddy doesn't like it when he knows you're hurting."

Spencer fought the bile that rose in his throat every time Sally referred to him as "Daddy." He might have spawned the two sniveling brats on her lap, but he never had been, nor would he ever be, their daddy.

Steering his truck onto the dirt-packed road leading to the Barnett farm, he was glad that Sally's folks had decided to drive on into Crawley after his old man's funeral. It would make leaving a whole lot easier. At least he wouldn't have her sad-eyed parents staring at him, much the way they'd done since the day he'd been forced to marry their daughter and move in with them.

When he parked the truck, he got out and, with a purposeful stride, walked toward the two-story house that he'd come to think of as his prison. He didn't stop to help Sally with the twins, nor did he look back to see if she followed him as he climbed the porch steps and opened the front door. Taking the stairs two at a time, he went straight to the bedroom he and Sally had shared since their wedding night and pulled a worn leather duffel bag from the top shelf of the closet.

"Spencer, what are you doing?" Sally asked, sounding out of breath. He supposed she was winded from carrying two babies up a flight of stairs without assistance.

He mentally shrugged as he stuffed clothes into the bag. It was one of many things she'd have to get used to doing without help.

"I'm leaving."

Just putting his intentions into words made him feel almost giddy from the relief coursing through him. He'd been waiting for this day from the moment his old man had forced him to marry Sally after learning Spencer had gotten her pregnant.

"Where are you going?" The sound of her quivering voice sent a chill up his spine much the way fingernails scraping a blackboard did.

"As far away from you and your whelps as I can get."

He knew his words cut her more deeply than any knife ever could. But he didn't care. She and her brats were the reason his plans for a better life had been put on hold for the past fifteen months.

Her broken sobs grated on his nerves and had him zipping the bag shut. To hell with the rest of his things.

He'd be buying new ones once he reached California, anyway.

Anxious to escape Sally and the wailing twins, he grabbed the bag and walked out of the room. He heard her footsteps behind him, but he didn't bother to look back. He never intended to look back.

He would try to stay in touch with his younger brother, though. Spencer was kind of fond of the kid.

But David had always been a bit of a sentimental fool about things. Even with the Ashton farm in foreclosure, and their old man dead from a heart attack because of it, the dumb kid had turned down Spencer's offer at the cemetery to go with him. David had said he couldn't imagine living anywhere but Nebraska and intended to make a fresh start in a new town—another godforsaken place just like Crawley.

When Spencer reached the door, Sally's words broke through his introspection, causing him to pause. "But these…are your children…Spencer. Don't they mean… anything to you?"

Turning, he gave her a disdainful smile as he watched her grip the newel post as if it might be the only thing keeping her on her feet. "Not a damn thing. As far as I'm concerned, you and your two squalling brats never existed."

Spencer watched her crumple into a pathetic, sobbing heap at the bottom of the stairs. Disgusted, he shook his head, then walked out the door and slammed it behind him.

He whistled a tune as he walked to his truck, threw the duffel bag on the seat, then slid behind the wheel. He was a free man now, and nothing was going to stop him from living the life he not only wanted but, without question, deserved.

One

Abigail Ashton stepped out of the carriage house, tilted her head back and enjoyed the morning sun bathing her face with its warm rays. California in February was light-years away from the weather she'd left behind in western Nebraska. When she'd flown out of the town of Scottsbluff yesterday morning, the temperature had been in the midteens and there was almost a foot of snow covering the ground. But here in Napa Valley, the temperature was a good forty degrees warmer and felt almost balmy in comparison.

No wonder her uncle had extended his stay in California. Even if his quest to meet with his father had thus far been futile, the weather was enough to tempt anyone.

Looking around at the neatly kept grounds of Lucas and Caroline Sheppard's estate, The Vines, Abby smiled. It had been extremely generous of Caroline to invite her and her Uncle Grant to stay with them for as long as they wanted to visit the Napa Valley area. All things considered, the woman had no reason to be kind to, or even like, them. After all, they had to be a painful reminder of Caroline's first marriage—to Abby's grandfather, Spencer Ashton. She shook her head in disgust. When he married Caroline, he'd conveniently failed to mention that he had a family he'd left behind in Nebraska, or that he hadn't bothered to divorce his first wife, Sally.

As Abby blindly stared across the dormant vineyard stretching out for acres behind the estate, her heart went out to Caroline. The woman hadn't so much as a clue that her marriage to Spencer had been illegal, until Uncle Grant showed up last month in hopes of meeting with his father for the first time in over forty years.

But even though she'd been shocked by the news, Caroline had been the epitome of class and graciousness. Once she'd learned that Uncle Grant was Spencer's son, she'd insisted that family was family and he needed to get acquainted with her children—his half siblings.

Abby bit her lower lip to keep it from trembling. She worried about Uncle Grant. He so wanted to confront his father and learn the reasons behind the abandonment of his first family. But the man simply refused to give Uncle Grant the time of day. For that matter, he refused to meet with Caroline's children, either.

Starting to walk toward the small lake behind the carriage house, Abby decided that she didn't care if she ever met her duplicitous grandfather. Anyone who could leave his young wife and eight-month-old twins in Nebraska, marry another woman in California without obtaining a divorce, then abandon that woman to marry his secretary and have yet another family wasn't worth knowing. Nor was he worth wasting time thinking about.

Besides, she would much rather concentrate on the fact that she was finally free. After working her tail off in school, she'd earned her degree, and she fully intended to enjoy every minute of the first vacation she'd had in years. Then, when she returned to Crawley, she'd be relaxed and ready to jump into her career with both feet.

A mixture of satisfaction and excitement coursed through her. By the end of spring, she'd realize the dream she'd had since she was twelve years old—she'd be practicing veterinary medicine in her own large-animal clinic.

Strolling down a path leading away from the carriage house, her mouth turned up in a smile when she spotted the stables not far from the small lake. Without missing a step, she headed straight for them. Painted white, with hunter green shutters, the building looked like a horse lover's paradise, and she couldn't wait to go inside.

The double doors on either end of the structure were open, allowing fresh air to flow through, and Abby didn't think twice about entering the shadowy interior. It took a moment for her eyes to adjust to the lower light, but when they did, her breath caught. The stable was everything she'd thought it would be. And more.

The bottom halves of the stalls were constructed of tongue-and-groove spruce boards, while the top halves had black grille front bars for maximum ventilation. Wide, split doors gave easy access to the enclosures and allowed the horses inside to appease their curiosity by hanging their heads over them when the top halves were swung back.

A beautiful blue roan gelding poked its head over the stall door as Abby walked by, and she stopped to rub the gentle animal's soft muzzle. As she scratched his broad forehead, she noticed that the inside walls of the stall were covered with a metal that resembled stainless steel and could easily be hosed down and disinfected. As a veterinarian and horse enthusiast, she was very impressed, and she highly approved of the Sheppards' choices for the welfare of their animals.

But as she stood there wishing she had the same setup at the farm in Nebraska, sudden movement at the far end of the stable caught her attention. As she watched, a man, wearing a wide-brimmed cowboy hat, chambray shirt and jeans, opened one of the stall doors to go inside. She couldn't help but think that he'd look more at home in a barn in Nebraska than in a stable in California wine country.

But her smile quickly faded and she forgot all about how out of place he looked when he led a beautiful dapple gray mare from the stall. The horse was limping badly, and it was obvious she had something wrong with her left hind leg.

"What seems to be the problem?" Abby asked, hurrying toward them.

Without looking her way, the man bent over to examine the mare. "I don't know how she did it, but Marsanne has managed to cut her fetlock."

"I'll take a look. I might be able to do something for her."

Shaking his head, he straightened to his full height. "I think we'd better leave it alone and let the vet take care of this one."

Abby caught her breath and her pulse skipped several beats when he turned to face her. The man standing on the other side of the mare wasn't just good-looking, he was heart-hammering gorgeous. With straight, dark-blond hair slipping from beneath his black Resistol to hang low on his forehead, a fashionable beard stubble covering his lean cheeks and startling blue eyes, he was without a doubt the best-looking cowboy she'd ever laid eyes on. Bar none.

When she realized that she must be staring at him like a schoolgirl with her first crush, she shook off her uncharacteristic reaction and walked around the horse to take a look at the injury. "Get the first-aid kit." Bending down beside the horse's hindquarters, she quickly assessed the wound. "The cut isn't as deep as it looks. It hasn't severed any of the ligaments or tendons, and won't need suturing." When she straightened, she glanced around the floor. There was a good drainage system, and it wouldn't be necessary to walk the horse outside to treat her. "Could you bring the hose over here? We'll need to cold rinse the wound to reduce the swelling before I apply a dressing."

"Now hold it right there, lady. You're not doing anything to this horse." Clearly annoyed, he walked around the mare to place his hands on Abby's shoulders, and, backing her away from the horse, he shook his head. "I'm going to call the vet and you're going to go back to the house, or wherever it is you came from."

His large hands on her shoulders sent a shiver of excitement up her spine, and she had to concentrate hard in order to ignore it. Luckily, it wasn't too difficult to do. He might be the best-looking guy she'd seen in all of her twenty-four years, but she wasn't the type to give in to anything as silly as attraction. Nor did she intend to be dismissed like so much fluff.

"I'm sorry, I didn't get your name," she said, careful to hide her irritation.

He dropped his hands to his sides. "Russ Gannon."

When he started to turn away, Abby placed her hand on his arm to stop him. Her breath lodged in her lungs at the feel of his hard muscles flexing beneath the blue fabric of his sleeve. She forced herself to ignore it and concentrate on the mare in need of treatment.

"It's nice to meet you, Russ. My name is Abigail Ashton. *Dr.* Abigail Ashton, DVM. But please call me Abby."

"You're a vet?" His skeptical expression told her that he still had his doubts about her treating one of the Sheppards' horses.

"More precisely, a large-animal veterinarian," she said, nodding. "Now, get the first-aid kit and a hose. I have a horse to treat."

Russ stared at the auburn-haired beauty barking orders at him like a drill sergeant. She sure didn't look like any of the veterinarians he'd ever met. Most of the ones he knew were men, and didn't have eyes the color of new spring grass or soft, feminine features that could easily grace the cover of a fashion magazine.

When she bent to look at the wound on Marsanne's

fetlock, the sight of her cute little upturned rear just about caused him to have a coronary. None of the vets he'd met had a figure that could stop traffic or remind him of just how long it had been since he'd been with a woman, either.

"Don't just stand there," she said impatiently. "This mare's fetlock needs treatment. And when you get the hose, bring some petroleum jelly and grease down her heel to keep it from getting sore."

Turning to get the hose and first-aid kit, he couldn't believe he was allowing this woman to order him around. He was used to giving orders, not taking them.

It had to be a case of shock. That's all he could think of that might explain his letting her order him around.

Where the hell had she come from, anyway? he wondered. He knew all of the Ashtons here at The Vines, and had heard about most of their relatives, but he couldn't recall them mentioning this one's name.

He shook his head as he gathered what she wanted. One thing was certain—if he'd ever met her, he damned sure would have remembered it. He had a weakness for redheads. And Dr. Abigail Ashton not only had hair the color of cinnamon and a killer body, she was an absolute knockout.

"What took you so long?" she asked when he returned with the requested items.

"Did anyone ever tell you you're a bossy little number?" he grumbled, handing them to her.

"My brother, Ford, tells me that all the time." Removing her jean jacket, she pushed the sleeves of her blue sweater up to her elbows, then tucked behind her ear a strand of hair that had escaped her ponytail. "Did anyone ever tell you that you're slower than molasses in January?"

Russ stared at her for a moment before he burst out laughing. It appeared that Abby Ashton could hold her own with the best of them.

"Now, what do you say we call a truce until after we get this mare on the road to recovery?" she asked, grinning.

His heart stalled and he had to take a deep breath to get it going again. When Abigail Ashton was issuing orders, she was awesome. But when she smiled, she was absolutely beautiful.

"What's the matter?" Her easy expression turned to one of concern. "You look like you were just treated to the business end of a cattle prod."

Damn! Was he that transparent? Apparently, he needed to make a trip into Napa and see if he could find a willing little filly to help him scratch the itch that he suddenly seemed to have developed.

"I'm fine," he lied.

"Good." She handed him the jar of petroleum jelly.

"Now, spread this over the mare's heel, then start running cold water on her leg so that it trickles down over the wound." She looked thoughtful for a moment. "Do you keep Epsom salts here in the stable?"

"Of course," he said, bending to coat the mare's heel with a good amount of the lubricant. "Do you intend to soak it or apply a hot compress after running cold water over the area?"

"I'm going to apply a hot compress in order to draw out bacteria." She paused. "By the way, do you have hot water out here, as well?"

Nodding, he stood up and handed her the jar of petroleum jelly. "I'll get it while you cold hose the mare's leg."

"That's not necessary," she said, smiling. "Just tell me where to find—"

"I'll take care of it," Russ said firmly.

He might not be as educated or refined as the Ashtons, but he did have manners. He wasn't about to stand by and watch a woman struggle with a heavy bucket of water.

Besides, he needed to put a little distance between them. Every time she turned her killer smile his way, certain parts of his body twitched and his heart felt like it was going to beat a hole in his rib cage.

He took a deep breath and did his best to regain his perspective. If he didn't get a hold on the situation, he just might have to use the cold water hose on himself.

* * *

An hour later, Russ watched Abby finish applying a poultice to the mare's fetlock, then wrap a bandage around it to hold it in place. Fortunately, Marsanne was a very well-mannered horse and tolerated the treatment without further injury to herself, Abby or him.

"I'll check on her again tomorrow morning and apply a fresh dressing, but I think she'll be fine," Abby said, standing up.

When she ran her hand along the horse's hindquarters, Russ swallowed hard. How would her delicate hands feel on his skin?

His heart slammed against his ribs. What the hell was wrong with him? He'd met her a little over an hour ago and he was fantasizing about her touching him?

Oh, brother, did he ever need that trip into town for a cold beer and a willing woman—and not necessarily in that order.

When she'd pulled the sleeves of her sweater back down to her wrists and shrugged into her blue jean jacket, she turned and stuck out her hand. "It was nice meeting you, Russ."

He automatically took her hand in his, but the moment their palms touched, he knew he'd made a serious error in judgment. An electric charge zinged up his arm, through his upper body, then traveled down to the region south of his belt buckle.

"I'll see you around," he managed, although he wasn't sure how the words made it through the cotton coating his throat.

"Are you feeling all right?" she asked, dropping his hand faster than he could blink. Her breathless tone and the pretty shade of pink coloring her creamy cheeks indicated that she'd felt it, too.

Good. At least he wasn't the only one suffering the unsettling sensation.

"Yeah, I'm fine," he said, fighting to keep from grinning. "How about you?"

She lifted her little chin and squared her slender shoulders as she started around him and the mare. "I couldn't be better."

Russ bit back a groan as he watched Abby walk the distance to the stable doors. The woman had legs that would tempt a eunuch. And his body was reminding him that was one thing he definitely was not.

Disgusted with himself and his own foolishness, he led Marsanne back into her stall, then headed toward the end of the stable where he kept his own horses, Blue and Dancer. Even if the woman was willing to indulge in a little vacation fun, he wasn't.

Number one, she was an Ashton, and his sense of loyalty and obligation just wouldn't allow him to disappoint Caroline or Lucas in any way. He snorted. And number two, what the hell could a book-smart beauty like Abby find appealing about a simple man with nothing more going for him than a knack for growing grapes and the ability to make the eight-second whistle when he rode bulls?

Two

"**T**hank you for the tour, Mercedes," Abby said, as she and Caroline's oldest daughter entered the Louret Vineyards tasting room.

Director of Marketing and Public Relations for the Sheppards' boutique winery, Mercedes Ashton smiled. "Oh, it's not over yet. The best is yet to come." She pointed to a small table by a floor-to-ceiling window. "Have a seat and I'll be right back."

Seating herself at the table Mercedes had indicated, Abby couldn't help but marvel at the ambience of the tasting room. The use of rich woods and muted lighting was extremely romantic, but the view of the vineyards from the narrow window was breathtaking. She could easily imagine herself staring out at the countryside somewhere in the south of France.

When Mercedes returned carrying a silver tray with cheese and samplings from the Louret award-winning reserve cellar, she grinned. "The best part of touring a winery is tasting the fruits of its labor."

After her new friend spent several minutes schooling her in the use of her senses to appreciate the clarity, bouquet and body of the wine, Abby shook her head as she reached for a piece of cheese. "I didn't realize there was such an art to tasting wine or that so much work went into the making of it."

Mercedes laughed. "It's more than just picking a few grapes and squeezing out the juice, that's for sure." She swirled the chardonnay in her glass. "Things are fairly quiet around here in winter. The wine is aging and there really isn't much going on beyond pruning the vines, maintenance on equipment and assessing which vines need to be replaced in the spring. Our busiest time of year is late summer and early fall, when the crush begins."

"Crush?" Abby was quickly learning that winemakers had their own language.

"The crush is what we call the harvest," Mercedes explained. "It starts when the grapes are picked and goes all the way through the process of making the wine. That's when Eli and Russ really get a workout."

"Russ Gannon?" Abby asked before she could stop herself.

Nodding, Mercedes gave her a curious glance. "You've met him?"

"Briefly." Abby shrugged and tried not to sound too interested. "He was in the stable this morning and I thought that's where he worked."

"It's a safe bet that's where you'll find him when he's not in the vineyards or off competing in a rodeo somewhere," Mercedes said, nodding. "But his official title is Vineyard Foreman. Russ is an absolute genius when it comes to growing things, and Eli relies on him for almost everything to do with the vines and during the crush."

"What's his event in rodeo?" Abby loved the sport and had even competed as a barrel racer a few times when she was in high school.

Mercedes looked thoughtful. "Russ doesn't talk about it, but I think Eli said he rides bulls." She paused. "But that's Russ. He doesn't talk about much of anything he does."

Abby grinned. "The mysterious type."

"Not really." Mercedes sighed. "Poor Russ. Life hasn't exactly been easy for him. His parents were killed in a car accident when he was only fifteen."

"Oh, how terrible," Abby gasped.

Although their circumstances were somewhat different, she knew what it was like to grow up without parents. Even before she'd abandoned her children, Grace Ashton had never been a mother to them, had never nurtured and cared for them the way a mother was supposed to. And, although her uncle Grant had loved her and her brother, and raised them as his own, it wasn't the same as having a mother and father.

"I feel so bad for him," she said, meaning it.

Mercedes nodded. "That's when he came to live with us. Lucas and Mr. Gannon had been best friends since grade school, and when Lucas found out that Russ had no family to turn to, he and Mother took Russ in."

"That was very kind of them." The more she learned about Caroline and Lucas Sheppard, the more she came to realize just how very special they were. "But that must have been devastating for him to lose both parents at the same time, and so tragically."

"I'm sure it was," Mercedes agreed, standing up to place their empty glasses on the tray. "Being older, I didn't become as close to him as my youngest brother, Mason. He's only a year younger than Russ and they became best friends."

"I don't think I've met Mason," Abby said, rising to help clear the table.

"He's in France studying new wine-making techniques," Mercedes said, laughing.

Abby waited for her to carry the serving tray over to

one of the uniformed attendants that Mercedes had referred to at the beginning of the tour as "wine educa-
tors." When she returned, they walked out a side door
and onto a path that led back to the mansion.

"Did I miss something?" Abby asked. "I don't
understand what's so funny about Mason studying in
France."

Mercedes's lips turned up slightly at the corners.
"You've always heard the old saying about someone trying to build a better mousetrap?"

"Let me guess," Abby laughed. "He's going to try to
make a better wine?"

"So he says." Mercedes smiled fondly and Abby could
tell that she adored her youngest brother. "But I think it's
just an excuse to backpack through France before he set-
tles into a position here at Louret with Eli and Russ."

"I'm sure that will make it easier for Russ to go to a
few more rodeos," Abby said before she could stop herself. Why did she keep mentioning him?

"Russ seems to have made a big impression on you."
Mercedes gave her a questioning look. "You wouldn't
happen to be interested, would you?"

"Good Lord, no!" Abby shook her head. "I don't
have time for him or any other man in my life."

"Really? He's a great guy and extremely good-looking. And, just for the record, available." From the twin-
kle in her eyes and the teasing tone of her voice, Abby

could tell that Mercedes wasn't the least bit convinced of her disinterest.

"I've worked too long and hard at getting my degree to become distracted now." As they walked onto the covered lanai at the back of the estate, she added, "Besides not having the time to become involved, Russ lives a thousand miles away. I'll be way too busy with my practice for a long-distance boyfriend."

"If you say so," Mercedes said, once again treating Abby to a knowing grin.

Realizing that she'd protested a little too much, it suddenly became clear that she wasn't trying to convince Mercedes as much as she was trying to convince herself. "I'm pretty tired," Abby said, suddenly needing time alone. "I think I'll take a nap before dinner." She hugged her new friend. "Thank you for the tour and wine tasting. I really enjoyed it."

"I'm glad." Mercedes hugged her back. "I probably won't see you at dinner this evening. I'm going out with a friend."

"Have a good time."

Turning to walk the short distance to the carriage house where she and her uncle were staying, Abby wondered what had gotten into her. Talking about Russ had been more unsettling than she could have ever imagined, and she needed time to get herself back on track.

All of her life she'd focused on her goal of becom-

ing a large-animal vet, studied her tail off in school and
made it happen. And along the way, she'd purposely
avoided becoming involved with anyone. It was a dis-
traction she didn't need and a chance she couldn't af-
ford to take. Her biggest fear had been, and probably
always would be, that she'd turn out to be just like her
mother—a man-crazed tramp who cared very little for
anyone or anything beyond her own selfish pursuits of
pleasure.

But the most disconcerting realization of all was that
when she and Mercedes had talked about Russ Gannon,
she couldn't seem to keep her pulse from skipping beats
or a funny, fluttery feeling from settling deep in the pit
of her stomach. When she'd found herself attracted to
boys in high school or college, she'd never experienced
anything even remotely close to what she felt when she
thought about Russ. And that bothered her. A lot.

Sighing, she entered the carriage house and climbed
the stairs. "You have serious issues, Abigail Ashton," she
muttered. "And at the moment, the biggest one is a
wine-making rodeo cowboy named Russ Gannon."

When Russ arrived at dawn a few days later to feed
the horses and muck out the stalls, he wasn't the least
bit surprised to see Abby already in the stable with her
sleeves rolled up, changing Marsanne's bandages. Three
out of the last four mornings, she'd arrived before him.

And whether he liked it or not, he'd started looking forward to their morning encounters.

"You're up even earlier than usual," he said, strolling over to where she bent down to change the dressing on the mare's fetlock.

Straightening, she gave him a smile that caused his pulse to take off like a racehorse out of the starting gate. He swallowed hard. She not only had auburn hair, she had his second biggest weakness—dimples. Why hadn't he noticed that before?

"When I'm at home, I'm used to getting up a lot earlier than this."

She brushed her hands off on the seat of her jeans and he almost groaned aloud. He'd love to run his hands over her sweet little rear.

Oblivious to his discomfort, she laughed and continued talking. "There's only two reasons a person sleeps late when they live on a farm—they're either too sick to get out of bed or it's snowing so hard they can't find the barn. And most of the time *that* doesn't even stop us."

"How often do you have blizzards?" he asked when he found his voice.

He didn't like the idea of her facing such harsh weather. But he was damned if he could figure out why it bothered him so much. She wasn't his to worry about, nor would she ever be.

"A blizzard moves through maybe once or twice a

year," she said, shrugging. "The rest of the time I'm up well before sunrise tending to my horses, then helping Uncle Grant, Ford and our hired hand, Buck, with the rest of the livestock."

"Cattle?"

She nodded as she bent to wrap a fresh bandage around the mare's lower leg. "We have a herd of about two hundred Black Angus."

"That sounds more like a ranch."

"Ranch or farm, whatever you want to call it." She finished securing the dressing, then stood up to face him. "When my great-grandparents owned it, they only had a few hundred acres. But when Uncle Grant took over, he bought up a couple of farms that were going under and now it's several thousand acres. We plant the majority in corn every year, as well as a couple thousand more that Uncle Grant leases. Then there's more than five hundred for pasturing the horses and cattle."

Russ couldn't help but be envious. He loved working the land and would give almost anything to have a place of his own to do just that.

Untying Marsanne to lead her out to the corral, he asked, "How many horses do you have?"

"Eight." She unrolled the sleeves of her jean jacket. "But only three of them are mine. The rest belong to Uncle Grant and Ford."

While Abby put the first-aid kit back together, he led

the gray mare out to the corral in order to muck out her stall. But when he returned, he found Abby already working at the task.

"Hey, you don't have to do that," he said, reaching for the pitchfork she held.

She shook her head and kept on forking the dirty straw into a wheelbarrow. "I don't mind. I'd rather be busy, anyway." Giving him a grin that made him weak in the knees, she added, "This vacation stuff is all right, but after a while it gets kind of boring."

Russ could understand her need to stay active. He'd never been able to stand being idle any longer than it took him to find something to do. "Well, if you're sure."

"I am." There was no hesitation, and Russ was certain that Abby meant what she said.

"Okay, while you finish up here, I'll turn the other horses and the pony out into the pasture, then bring back fresh straw."

By the time he returned, he found that Abby had mucked out three of the stalls and was ready to start on another one. "You work fast," he said, taking the pitchfork from her, "but it's my turn. Why don't you take it easy for a while?"

"But I don't mind," she argued.

He liked ambition in a woman, but he wasn't about to stand around while she did all the work. "I'll make you a deal. You go up to The Vines and have breakfast.

Then, after you eat, come back out here and we'll take my horses for a ride."

Her pretty, emerald eyes lit up, and she gave him a grin that made his heart thump his rib cage. "You've got yourself a deal, cowboy. What time?"

"Time?" How was he supposed to think when she was looking at him that way? Hell, he was lucky to remember his own name.

"When do you want me to come back out here?" she asked patiently.

"Whenever you get finished with breakfast will be fine." He was definitely going to have to stay focused when Abby was around. Otherwise, she was going to think he was a complete fool.

"I'll be back in a flash," she said, hurrying down the wide aisle.

As he watched her pretty little backside disappear through the open doors at the far end of the stable, Russ let out the breath he was pretty sure he'd been holding since he'd walked in and found her working on the mare. Damn, but the woman could send his blood pressure into stroke range with nothing more than a smile. And that's what made her dangerous.

Stabbing the pitchfork into the straw, he gazed off into space. He wasn't looking for a relationship. Especially not with a woman who lived a thousand miles away. His life was here, working for Lucas and Caroline Sheppard. And even though they'd never asked him for anything, and had always tried to make him feel a part of their family, he felt an obligation to them for taking him in after his folks died.

He took hold of the pitchfork and began forking dirty straw into the wheelbarrow.

Besides, Abby would be returning to Nebraska in another week or so to start her veterinary practice and resume her life on the family farm. And that was the way it was supposed to be.

But it didn't mean they couldn't have a good time and enjoy each other's company for as long as she visited Napa Valley, did it? He could show her around and she could tell him more about her life in Nebraska and all that land he'd love to work.

Satisfied that he'd come up with a solution they could both live with, he whistled a tune as he finished mucking out the stalls. There was no chance of either of them being hurt as long as there was no emotional investment.

A smile tugged at the corners of his mouth. As long as he kept that in mind, they'd both be just fine.

Russ's lower body tightened when he watched Abby put her foot in the stirrup and swing up into the saddle on Dancer's back. The sight of her jeans pulled tightly over her sweet little rump, and her long slender legs straddling the gelding, had him wondering why he'd thought taking her for a ride was such a good idea. All he could think about was how her legs would feel wrapped around him as he sank himself deep—

"How old are your horses?" she asked, breaking into his erotic thoughts.

"Dancer is five," Russ said, mounting the blue roan. He shifted in the saddle to keep from emasculating himself. "I sometimes use him to haze steers for a couple of friends who compete in steer wrestling." He patted the roan's neck. "And Blue is six. I used to do a little team roping on him."

She smiled as they rode away from the stables. "Mercedes said you rode bulls, but she failed to mention that you rope, too. How often do you compete?"

Abby had been asking some of the Ashtons about him? The thought pleased him more than he could have imagined.

"I try to make as many rodeos as work around the vineyard permits." He chuckled. "The rest of the time, I have to be content with riding Blue and Dancer around here."

"Are they both registered with the Quarter Horse Association?"

"Yep." He wasn't surprised that Abby knew what breed they were. Considering her background with animals, she'd naturally recognize the classic traits of the breed. "Dancer's full name is Stormy Jack Dancer, and Blue's is Diablo's Blue Lightning."

"Beautiful names for beautiful animals," she murmured.

They rode in silence for several minutes and Russ found himself admiring the easy way Abby sat a horse. Relaxed and confident, he could tell she'd spent many hours in the saddle.

"What about your horses? What breed are they?" he asked.

"Mostly mixed. Magic is a quarter-horse-and-Arabian mix gelding. He's the one I ride the most. Then there's my mare, Angel. She's mostly quarter horse, but we're not sure about the rest of her bloodlines." Abby laughed. "She's the product of Uncle Grant's mare giving a come-hither look over the fence to our nearest neighbor's stallion."

An electric charge zinged up his spine at the sound of her soft voice and delightful laughter. He had to clear the rust out of his throat before he could speak. "I thought you said you had three horses."

She nodded. "The third one is a mustang I adopted from the BLM a few years ago. His name is Crazy Horse."

"I've heard about the Bureau of Land Management's Adopt-A-Horse program. Did you name him after the Native American chief?"

"No. He's a crazy horse." Laughing, she shook her head. "Ford named him because Crazy gives a whole new meaning to the word *wild*. Like all mustangs, he's rebellious and distrustful, and I'm the only one he's ever let get near him. But I love him even though I know he'll never be tame enough to ride."

"It sounds like you really enjoy living on the farm," Russ said, reining Blue in.

"I do." She brought Dancer to a halt beside him. "Living out on the prairie has its downside when the temperatures drop and the windchill feels like you've been transported to the Arctic, or it gets so hot and humid in the summer that you feel like you're in a sauna. But I really couldn't imagine living anywhere else."

They'd ridden around the entire vineyard and back to the small lake a hundred or so yards behind the stables. "Do you want to sit and talk for a while?" he asked.

"Sure."

When they'd dismounted, they ground tied the two horses and walked over to sit beneath a grove of oak trees at the water's edge.

"What about you, Russ? Have you always lived in Napa Valley?"

He lowered himself to sit beside her on the carpet of grass. "No. Until I was fifteen, I lived about a hundred and fifty miles north of here, on a ranch outside of Red Bluff."

"I'm so sorry about your parents," she said, placing her hand on his arm. "Mercedes said that you lost them in a car accident."

The warmth of her hand through his shirtsleeve, and the sincere tone of her voice, caused a tightness in his chest. "That was eleven years ago," he said, nodding. "Lucas brought me here right after Mom and Dad's funeral, and I've lived here ever since." They sat in silence for some time before he asked, "What about your parents, Abby? I've heard you talk about your brother and uncle, but I've never heard you mention your mom and dad."

"That's because there isn't a whole lot to talk about." He could tell it wasn't a pleasant subject for her.

"I'm sorry," he said, wishing he'd kept his mouth shut. "I didn't mean to pry."

He watched her pluck a blade of grass and shred it into strings, then toss it aside and pluck another. "I don't mind talking about it, exactly," she finally said. "It's just that it's rather embarrassing to have to tell someone that your mother was the town tramp and you have no clue who your father is."

Russ wasn't sure what he'd expected her to say, but it certainly hadn't been that. "That's a pretty harsh thing to say about the woman who gave you life, honey."

"But it's the truth." She didn't look at him when she continued, but he could tell she was embarrassed by the heightened color on her cheeks. "Grace was sixteen when she got pregnant with my brother, and eighteen when she had me. But she never would tell our great-grandparents or Uncle Grant who our father—or fathers—were." She sighed. "That in itself is no big deal. But Grace made sure we knew that she didn't want us. She always told us that if our great-grandparents hadn't insisted that she stay and take responsibility for us, she'd have left Crawley as soon as she found a way out."

"Your mother and uncle were raised by their grand-parents?" Russ had never known anything but love from his parents, and it was hard for him to grasp that a woman had been so callous toward her own children.

"My great-grandparents finished raising Grace and Uncle Grant after their mother, Sally, died of cancer," Abby said, nodding. "They were twelve."

"I know from experience that losing a parent isn't easy," Russ said gently. "It can bring out a rebellious streak in some people."

"That might have been the case if Grace had been someone else, but I can never remember a time when she acted as though we actually meant anything to her." She shrugged one slender shoulder. "Uncle Grant told us that she was just like their father, Spencer. He's nar-cissism personified, and so was his daughter."

"You talk about her like she isn't around anymore," Russ said, reaching out to take Abby's hand in his.

"She isn't." She stared off across the lake. "Grace abandoned me and Ford when I was six and he was eight. But we were lucky—Uncle Grant loved us and finished raising us as his own." Her fond smile was evidence of how much she loved the man. "He's always been more of a father to us than an uncle."

The more Russ heard about Grace Ashton, the more he understood why Abby didn't like talking about her. "Where did your mother go?"

Abby's laughter held little humor. "Who knows? She went to the store one day and just didn't bother coming home. We're almost certain that she ran off with a sales representative who made frequent visits to the Crawley General Store."

"Do you know his name? Maybe if you find out where he is, you'd be able to track her down."

"His name is Wayne Cunningham, but that's about all we know." Brushing a strand of hair from her porcelain cheek, she turned her gaze back to him. "Uncle Grant checked with the company Wayne worked for, but that was a dead end. They were looking for him, too. It turns out that he disappeared at the same time as Grace, and without bothering to turn in the money from his latest sales."

"Real nice guy," Russ said, unable to hold back his sarcasm. He'd tried all of his life not to be judgmental, but this was one time he couldn't help himself. "It sounds to me like your mom got hold of a real loser when she hooked up with this Wayne character."

Abby nodded. "Uncle Grant doesn't have much to say about it, but Ford and I think they probably deserve each other."

"I'm sorry for the way it all turned out, honey," Russ said, pulling her into his arms.

He'd only meant the gesture to be comforting, but the feel of Abby's soft, feminine body pressed to his chest sent a shock wave straight through him, and his good intentions took a hike. He could no more stop himself from kissing her than he could stop the sun from setting in the west.

Three

Gazing into Abby's pretty, emerald eyes, Russ slowly lowered his mouth to hers. The feel of her soft lips had his heart thumping inside his chest like a sultry jungle drum. But when she tentatively moved to bring her arms up to circle his neck, then tangled her fingers in the hair at his nape, his pulse took off at a gallop.

He lightly traced the seam of her mouth with his tongue, and when she parted for him on a soft sigh, Russ slipped inside. As he stroked her inner recesses, her sweet taste and shy response sent his blood pressure soaring and brought his neglected hormones to full alert.

Without breaking the kiss, he lowered her to the soft grass and partially covered her body with his. She felt so damned good beneath him. In twenty-six years of life, he'd never wanted a woman as quickly or as fiercely as he wanted Abby at that very moment.

Parting her legs with one of his, he pressed his thigh against her feminine warmth as he eased his hand inside her jean jacket to cup her breast. Rewarded by her soft moan of pleasure, he chafed the peak with his thumb through the layers of her clothing.

His body hardened predictably, and he allowed her to feel what she was putting him through, how she made him want her. But a split second later, he felt her go perfectly still, then push against his chest.

"Please stop," she said, her tone clearly bordering on panic.

Russ immediately removed his hand and untangled their legs to help her sit up. "What's wrong?" He didn't think he'd gotten so carried away that he'd hurt her. And he was sure she'd enjoyed what he'd been doing.

"I…have to go." She scrambled to her feet, and before he could stop her, she ran over to where Dancer grazed a few feet away.

Bewildered, Russ watched her quickly mount the gelding, then rein the horse toward the stable. Jumping to his feet, he caught Blue's reins and swung up into the saddle to follow her. But Abby had nudged Dancer into a gallop and was already disappearing around the side of the building.

When he reached the double doors, Russ dismounted and led Blue inside. He wasn't sure what the problem was, but he damned sure intended to find out.

"Abby, what happened out there?"

"Please, not now." She didn't look at him as she continued to remove Dancer's saddle.

He noticed that her hand shook slightly when she picked up the brush to groom the bay, and, reaching out, he started to take it from her. "I'll see to the horses," he said gently. When she flinched and pulled back, he let his hand drop to his side. "Abby, honey, talk to me. What's wrong?"

"I rode him. I'll take care of brushing him down," she said, ignoring his question and turning back to Dancer.

For the next several minutes, they worked in uneasy silence as they groomed the horses. Russ suspected Abby's sudden panic might have something to do with what she'd told him about her mother. But if she wouldn't talk to him, he had no way of finding out if that was what bothered her, or if it was something else.

When she finished brushing Dancer, she led him to his stall, then started toward the open doors at the end of the stable. "Thank you for letting me ride your horse," she said as she walked past him.

"Abby, we need to talk." He placed his hand on her shoulder.

She didn't look at him, but he felt her body stiffen a moment before she sidestepped his touch and continued walking. "There's nothing to say."

Russ waited until she'd disappeared through the double doors before he cut loose with a string of cuss words that could have blistered paint. Abby might think there was nothing to discuss, but he sure as hell did. And when she arrived tomorrow morning to take care of the dressing on Marsanne's fetlock, he had every intention of being here, waiting for her.

Just as she'd done for the past three mornings, Abby waited until she was sure Russ had finished tending the horses and gone to the winery to work with Eli before she walked down to the stables to check on the gray mare. She knew it was the coward's way of dealing with how she'd acted the day he'd kissed her, but she really didn't know any other way to handle the situation.

She didn't want to have to explain to Russ why she'd panicked. It was too embarrassing to admit that her mother's reputation around Crawley had forced her to prove, time and again, that she wasn't cut from the same cloth. Nor was she eager to tell him that she'd had intimacy issues since almost losing her virginity when she was fifteen, simply because her date for the homecoming dance didn't believe that Grace Ashton's daughter meant what she said when she'd told him "no."

Kicking a pebble, Abby watched it skitter to the edge of the path. Whether it was fair or not, she'd been having to live down the sins of her mother from the time she was old enough for boys to notice her. That's why she'd finally just given up dating and concentrated on finishing school early.

But when Russ had kissed her, she'd encountered a problem she'd never had to deal with before—she hadn't wanted him to stop. And that's what bothered her. She'd wanted him to hold her close, to touch her in ways she'd never been touched. That had been the sole reason for her uncharacteristic panic attack.

What made being with Russ different? Could she really be like Grace after all?

As she entered the stable and walked down the aisle toward the tack room, Abby decided there were no easy answers. She had a feeling that, unlike Grace, not just any man could make her feel the way Russ did. Unfortunately, she couldn't risk finding out why his kiss made her burn in ways that she'd never even imagined. If she did take the chance, she might learn things about herself that she'd rather not know.

"I was wondering when you were going to show up."

Lost in her disturbing thoughts, Abby jumped. "What

are you doing here? Aren't you supposed to be working in the winery?"

Russ was sitting on a bench in the tack room, close to the cabinet where the medical supplies were stored, his legs stretched out in front of him with his boots crossed at the ankles. He looked relaxed, confident and sexier than any man had a right to look.

Smiling, he used his thumb to push up the wide brim of his Resistol, then shook his head. "I decided to take the day off."

"Why?" She didn't mean to sound so blunt, but she found it extremely disconcerting to have the object of her thoughts appear seemingly out of nowhere.

He shrugged. "I have some unfinished business to take care of."

She stepped over his legs to get to the storage cabinet. "Then why aren't you off somewhere taking care of it?"

His smile caused her knees to feel as if the tendons had been replaced with rubber bands. "Now that you're here, I can."

"I can't imagine why my being here makes any difference," she lied as she reached inside the cabinet.

"You're my unfinished business, honey."

She laughed nervously. "I have no idea why on earth you'd think we have business to settle."

Her breath caught when he rose to his feet, placed

both hands on her shoulders and turned her to face him. "Don't play dumb with me, Abby. We both know you're too smart for that."

With Russ standing only inches away, she found it extremely hard to catch her breath. "I don't think this is a good idea."

"I do." His easy expression had been replaced with one of unwavering determination. "I want to know why you ran when I kissed you."

She stared into his deep blue gaze for several seconds before she shrugged out of his grasp to turn back to the cabinet. "You wouldn't understand." Finding the supplies she needed, she brushed past him to walk out into the wide stable aisle.

Before she could take more than a couple of steps, he caught her by the arm. "I understand a whole lot more than you think I do." Cupping her cheek with his palm, he tilted her head, forcing her to look at him. The tenderness she saw in his eyes caused her chest to tighten. "Do you want to know why I think you got so upset, Abby?"

"No."

"You're afraid," he said as if she hadn't spoken.

Shaking her head, she laughed, but the sound was hollow even to her own ears. "That's where you're wrong, cowboy."

"Really?" The look on his face warned her that he intended to prove her a liar. "Then let me kiss you, Abby."

A mixture of excitement and panic coursed through her. "This is ridiculous."

"You're not your mother," he said, gently pulling her into his arms.

Suddenly feeling defeated, she didn't have the strength to resist. God help her, she didn't even want to. She wanted Russ to hold her close, wanted him to kiss her again. "But what if you're wrong?"

"Believe me, I'm not." His reassuring smile as he lowered his mouth to hers sent a shiver up her spine. "Not about this."

When his firm lips covered hers, Abby tried to remain impassive, to prove to herself as much as to Russ that she was unaffected. But the tender way he traced her lower lip with his tongue, and the masculine taste of him when he coaxed her to open for him, quickly had her forgetting her resolve not to let it happen again.

Dropping the bandaging supplies, she curled her fingers in the fabric of his shirt and held on for dear life. The feel of his hard muscles beneath the chambray, and the steady beat of his heart, caused tingles of excitement to race up her spine and her knees to give way. When he slipped his tongue inside to explore and tease, a sweet warmth began to flow through her veins and a delicious fluttery feeling settled deep in the pit of her stomach.

She'd been kissed before, but never like this. Never with such mind-shattering tenderness or such mastery.

Abby couldn't stop a tiny moan of pleasure from escaping when Russ tightened his arms around her and aligned her body to his. The feel of his hard male frame against her softer feminine one sent a streak of longing throughout her entire body, and without a thought, she melted against him.

But when she became aware of his insistent arousal pressed to her lower belly, the heat coursing through her began to form a tight coil of need deep in the very core of her. And it scared her as little else could.

Pulling back, she shook her head. "R-Russ…I can't—"

"It's all right, honey." He allowed her to put space between them, but continued to hold her in the circle of his arms. "I'm not going to lie to you, Abby. I want you. But it's never been my style to force myself on a woman. And I'm not about to start now."

The sincerity in his brilliant blue eyes took her breath. She had no doubt he meant what he said. But what she was feeling at the moment wasn't his problem. It was hers.

"I know that. You're name isn't Harold." She hadn't intended to say the name of the boy who'd taken her to homecoming her sophomore year. Hoping Russ hadn't noticed, she hurried to add, "I'm the one I'm worried will do something stupid."

"Whoa. Back up just a minute. Who's Harold?"

Abby closed her eyes and took a deep breath. She should have known Russ would pick up on her blunder. "He was my date for a dance in high school. But that's not important."

"I disagree." His brow furrowed into a deep frown. "Did he try to—"

"Yes, but he decided differently."

Russ's frown deepened. "What changed his mind?"

The man was as tenacious as a bulldog going after a juicy bone. "Are you always this nosy?"

"Are you always this evasive?" His expression softened. "Tell me what happened, honey."

She sighed. It was clear Russ wasn't going to give up. "When I told him 'no,' Harold tried to force the issue. But my knee to his groin convinced him otherwise." She shook her head. "When I walked away, he was writhing on the ground, moaning and looking like he was going to throw up."

Russ winced as if he knew what Harold must have been feeling. "I can't say that he didn't get what he deserved. But damn, I'll bet that hurt like hell."

"I'm sure it did." Abby wasn't happy or proud of what she'd had to do. She didn't like hurting anything or anyone. But she wasn't going to be a victim if it was within her power to prevent it. "I'm sorry I had to hurt him, but it must have taught him a lesson. He never bothered me again."

Russ laughed. "I can't say I blame him."

She bit her lip in an effort to keep from smiling. "In fact, he refused to be anywhere near me unless there was a group of people around."

Russ's expression turned serious. "Abby, I give you my word that you'll never have to worry about something like that happening with me. I promise not to touch you unless you tell me to."

Staring into his steady blue gaze, she saw nothing but sincerity and she knew she could trust him to maintain his control no matter how heated the moment became. "Like I said before, it's not you I'm worried about."

He shook his head. "I don't think you have to be concerned about you, either. From what you've told me about your mother, and what I know about you, you're nothing like her."

"I hope not."

Releasing her, he bent to pick up the dressings for the gray mare. When he straightened and handed them to her, he smiled. "Have dinner with me tonight, Abby."

"I don't know—"

"I promise it will be just a couple of friends getting together for the evening. Nothing more."

"I don't even know where you live." Was she actually considering his offer?

"I live in the guest cottage on the other side of the lake." He opened the stall's half door and led the mare out into the wide aisle. "And I make great spaghetti and meatballs."

Abby weighed her options as she bent to assess the wound on the horse's fetlock. Uncle Grant had plans for the evening and Mercedes had another date with her boyfriend, Craig. Did she really want to spend the evening alone in the carriage house watching television?

Straightening, Abby shook her head. "I don't think we'll have to continue dressing it. The wound is almost completely healed."

"That's great." He led the mare back into her stall, then, securing the door, turned to face Abby. "Now, what about dinner? I could come by for you around seven."

She took a deep breath and made her decision. "Don't bother. I'll walk."

When he heard the knock on the front door, Russ wiped his hands on a towel and walked over to open it. The sight of Abby standing on the small porch, her dark auburn hair down around her shoulders, robbed him of breath. She was one of the most beautiful women he'd ever had the privilege to meet, and unless he missed his guess, she didn't even know it.

"You're just in time to help with the salad while I drain the spaghetti." He could tell she was nervous, and wanting to put her at ease, he grinned. "If I try to toss the damned stuff, we'll be sweeping it off the floor."

"What makes you think I can do any better?" she asked, laughing.

The delightful sound caused a warm feeling to spread throughout his chest. "You're a wo—"

"Watch it, buster." Her dimples appeared when she smiled. "You're about to get in over your head."

His heart stalled and he wasn't sure it would ever beat again. She had his two biggest weaknesses—red hair and dimples—and the evening was going to be a true test of his control.

Clearing the rust from his throat, he tried to remember what they'd been talking about. "I was just going to tell you that you're a woman…who should sit down and rest while I toss the salad."

"Good save, cowboy." She laughed as she walked into his tiny kitchen, picked up the two oversize wooden forks and began tossing the salad. "Not that I believe for a minute that's what you intended to say."

They worked side by side in companionable silence for several minutes—he putting the finishing touches on the spaghetti and she filling salad plates and setting the table.

"Would you like some wine?" he asked, holding the chair for her at the small, wooden kitchen table.

She shook her head. "I have to confess that I'm not much of a wine connoisseur. I normally drink water or iced tea with my meals."

"Don't feel bad, honey." He laughed. "I never touch the stuff, either."

Her expressive eyes widened. "But you make wine for a living."

Reaching into the refrigerator, he brought out a pitcher of tea, poured them each a glass, then sat down opposite her. "When I drink, which isn't all that often, I prefer beer."

She lifted her glass. "Here's to wine-making, beer-drinking, rodeo cowboys."

Grinning, he touched his glass to hers. "And to beautiful, large-animal vets with attitude."

They talked over dinner and Russ learned about Abby's brother, Ford, developing a highly successful cattle feed while he was still in college. He'd leased the patented formula to several major feed companies and now the product was distributed not only in the States, but in several foreign countries, as well.

"Is he still in development?" Russ asked.

"No. Ford's an independent consultant to large cattle breeders, now." She grinned. "And when he's not in some other part of the country tromping through somebody's feedlot, he's out in our fields working on his tan."

The reappearance of Abby's dimples caused the air to lodge in Russ's lungs, and he had to concentrate hard on what she'd said. "There's nothing wrong with that. In July and August, when the temperature hits the upper nineties around here, I've been known to take my shirt off while I work in the vineyards."

"I thought the weather in Napa Valley was mild all the time," she said, placing her fork on the edge of her plate.

"It is." As if to contradict him, lightning flashed outside, followed by the rumble of thunder.

They both laughed.

"Well, most of the time the weather's nice," he said, rising to take their plates to the sink. "I baked an apple pie for dessert. Would you like some now or do you want to wait and have it with coffee later?"

"You made a pie? I'm impressed."

Turning to face her, he gave her a sheepish grin. "I didn't say I made it. Just baked it."

"Oh, I see." Her smile sent his blood pressure soaring and had him wondering if he'd be able to keep the promise he'd made her earlier in the afternoon. "I think having pie with coffee later would be nice."

He nodded. "Sounds good to me. I'll start the coffeemaker." A sudden flash of lightning illuminated the room a split second before thunder rattled the plates in the sink and everything went completely dark. "Or not."

She laughed, and the sound sent a shaft of longing straight up his spine and had him deciding that he'd been a complete fool for promising to keep his hands to himself. "I think we'll be eating that pie by candlelight," she said.

"Looks like it," he agreed, cursing himself for not thinking of using candles during dinner. It appeared he needed to brush up on his dating techniques, he decided as he opened the drawer where he kept a flashlight, candles and an odd assortment of small tools.

But as he pulled two fat, red candles from the drawer and set them on saucers to light the wicks, he wondered who the hell he was kidding. How often did he entertain a woman at the cottage? And especially one like Abby? Hell, he could count on one hand the number of times he'd even been out with a woman who had a college education, let alone one with a doctorate.

"Let's sit in the living room," he said, leading the way into the small sitting area. "The power will probably be back on in a few minutes."

At least, he hoped it would. Sitting on the couch with a beautiful woman in the romantic glow from the candles was not going to be easy on his libido.

"I'm used to the electricity going off," Abby said, sitting beside him. "In winter, our power lines snap from the cold, and in spring and summer, winds from thunderstorms tear them down."

"We don't have outages that often," he said, wondering what on earth he'd been thinking when he'd asked her to dinner. In about two seconds they were going to exhaust talking about the weather. Then what? He had a few ideas, but all of them involved her in his arms.

Damn! He should have known that promise not to touch her until she told him to was going to come back and bite him in the butt.

"When are you competing again?" she asked, breaking into his morose thoughts.

"This weekend, down in Wild Horse Flats." He shrugged. "It's a small rodeo about three hundred and fifty miles south of here, but I always do well there."

She gave him a smile that made his heart pound. "Sometimes the smaller rodeos are the most fun."

"You like watching rodeo?"

She nodded. "When we were in high school, I used to do a little barrel racing and Ford competed as a calf roper at some of the ones around Crawley."

He lifted his arm to put it on the back of the couch behind her shoulders, then dropped it back onto his thigh—she might think he was going back on that damned promise.

"Why did you stop competing?"

"I had to make a choice between taking summer classes to finish school early or doing something fun. I chose school." She gave him an odd look. "Were you going to put your arm around me?"

He cleared his throat. "Actually, I was going to rest it along the back of the couch, but—"

Her eyes widened. "Don't you think you're taking what you said this afternoon to the extreme?"

"Not really."

He'd keep his word, even if it killed him. And with her sitting so close, it just might.

"Well, I do." She shifted on the couch to face him. "You mean you aren't even going to try to kiss me?"

He shook his head. "I gave you my word. The only way I'll touch you is if you tell me to."

Abby stared at Russ for several long seconds, her heart hammering against her ribs for all it was worth. Could she really be that forward? Did she have the nerve to tell him that she wanted him to modify his promise?

After walking back to the carriage house, she'd spent the rest of the afternoon thinking about what he'd told her. And he was right—she wasn't her mother, nor was she anything like her.

Grace Ashton was weak-willed, hedonistic and selfish. But her daughter was a strong, capable woman who was just coming into her own. A woman who was learning to trust her instincts and determine exactly what she wanted. And heaven help her, at the moment she wanted Russ to hold her, wanted him to kiss her like she'd never been kissed before.

But he'd made that dumb promise and she was going to have to do something she wasn't exactly comfortable with. She was either going to have to ask him to kiss her, or she was going to have to kiss him.

Deciding that action spoke louder than words, her heart skipped a beat when she leaned forward and pressed her lips to his. She'd never in all of her twenty-four years done anything like this, but as she nibbled at his firm, warm mouth, she found the experience extremely exciting and, to a degree, liberating.

When he groaned and shifted toward her, she expected him to put his arms around her and take over. But other than kissing her back, he just sat there. Apparently, Russ was waiting for her to verbalize what she wanted.

She leaned back and noticed that both of his hands were balled into tight fists at his sides. He wanted to hold her as badly as she wanted to be held. But he wasn't going to make a move until she let him know that she was ready for him to take an active role.

"Russ?"

"What, Abby?" His eyes were still closed and he sounded as if he was having trouble breathing.

"Will you please touch me?"

Four

Abby watched Russ's eyes fly open a moment before he groaned and reached out to pull her into his arms. "Good Lord, woman, I thought you'd never ask."

"I have something else I want you to do." A shiver raced up her spine at the feel of his hard body pressed to hers.

"What's that, honey?" he asked, nuzzling the side of her neck.

"I want you to forget about that promise."

She felt him go perfectly still a moment before he drew back to look at her. His expression was a mixture of relief and confusion.

"Are you sure?"

Taking a deep breath, she nodded. "I'll let you know if something makes me nervous or uncomfortable."

"That works for me." He lightly kissed her cheek. "But do me a favor."

Her skin tingled where his lips had been. "And that would be?"

"Just keep in mind that I'm not Harold." Giving her a grin that made her stomach flutter, he added, "All you have to do is tell me no. It doesn't take a knee to the groin to get my attention."

"I'll remember that," she said, putting her arms around his wide shoulders. "Now, kiss me like you mean it, cowboy."

His wicked grin caused her insides to quiver. "I aim to please, ma'am."

Abby's heart raced and her stomach felt as if it did a backflip when he slowly lowered his mouth to cover hers. Circling his neck with her arms, she savored the feel of his firm lips teasing hers, reveled in the contrast of their bodies. Honed by years of physical labor, Russ had muscles strong enough to crush her, yet he held her to him as gently as if he held a small child.

But when he slipped his tongue inside to stroke hers with infinite care, she ceased to think and tentatively met him halfway. As she tasted and explored him as he did her, she was rewarded with his groan of pleasure, and a feminine power that she'd never experienced before began to fill her. For the first time in her life, she was exploring her own sexuality, beginning to understand what it meant to be a woman. And she loved it.

A tremor passed through his big body a moment before he broke the kiss and lifted her to sit on his lap. "Honey…we'd better stop…before this goes any…further," he said, sounding completely out of breath.

His hard arousal pressing against her backside caused an answering tightness to form deep in her belly and a spark of need to skip along every nerve ending in her body. Scooting off his lap to sit beside him, she decided that she'd tested her newfound freedom as far as she was comfortable with for one night.

"Thank you for dinner, but it's getting late and I should probably go." She listened to the gently falling rain outside. "Do you think you could drive me back to the carriage house?"

"Sure," he said, nodding. "But we'll have to wait a minute or two."

"Why?"

His deep chuckle sent a wave of goose bumps shimmering over her skin. "At the moment, I don't think I have enough blood north of my belt buckle to keep from passing out when I stand up."

Her cheeks heated, and for the first time in her life, she couldn't think of a thing to say.

Reaching out, his smile faded as he threaded his fingers through her hair, then cupped the back of her head and pulled her forward for a quick kiss. "Go to the rodeo down in Wild Horse Flats with me this weekend, Abby."

She stared at him for endless seconds. "Russ, I'm not sure that would be a good idea."

Why was she hesitating? Why wasn't she telling him "no" outright?

He shook his head and placed his index finger to her lips. "We'll leave here on Friday and be back Monday. And in case you're wondering about the sleeping arrangements, my horse trailer has living quarters with two beds." Kissing her again, he rose to his feet and held his hand out to help her from the couch. "Just think about it. You can let me know your answer later in the week."

"Uncle Grant, I haven't heard you mention much about the Spencer situation in the past few days," Abby said over breakfast the next morning. "How are things going with that?"

Looking over the rim of his coffee cup, her uncle shrugged. "About the same. He refuses to meet with me or any of the other Ashtons from here at The Vines."

His obsession with meeting his father was beginning to concern her. "What are you going to do?"

"Wait him out." He gave her a fatherly smile. "I have a meeting this morning with Cole and Eli to discuss our options. If we're lucky, we'll come up with something to prompt Spencer to meet with us. They'd like their questions answered, too. One of the ideas we've come up with is having me go to the media with the story."

"Do you think that will work?" she asked, clearing their empty plates to put them in the sink.

For the past few mornings, she'd prepared breakfast for the two of them in the carriage house. It was really the only time they'd found to talk.

Her uncle nodded. "I hope so. I doubt that he'd want his business associates to know that he was guilty of bigamy, or that he gained control of the Lattimer Corporation by means of fraud." He smiled. "But I don't want you worrying about it, Abby. Things will work out for the best."

"I hope so," she said, praying he was right. Uncle Grant deserved answers from the man who'd deserted him all those years ago.

"But enough about me." He motioned for her to sit down and finish her coffee. "I have a few minutes before I'm supposed to meet with Cole and Eli. Tell me what you've been up to, Sprite."

His use of the nickname he'd given her when she was small caused her heart to swell with love for the man who had sacrificed so much at such an early age for her and her brother. Her uncle had only been twenty-four when his sister walked out and left him to raise her two children. But Abby could never remember a single time that she'd heard him complain or express any regrets for the way his life had turned out. He'd never married and, although he hadn't said as much, she suspected that he'd given her and Ford his undivided attention in an attempt to make up for the lack of love from Grace.

"There's really not much to tell," she said. "Mercedes gave me a tour of the winery the other day and tried to educate me in the fine art of wine tasting." Grinning, she added, "And I've come to a conclusion about that."

"Really?"

She nodded. "I've decided that wine must be an acquired taste."

He laughed. "That's true. Anything else going on?"

"Other than treating one of the horses down at the stable for a lacerated fetlock, I really haven't been doing a lot," she said, trying to decide if she should bring up Russ asking her to go to the rodeo in Wild Horse Flats with him.

Normally, she discussed everything with her uncle, listened to his opinion, then made her decisions. But going away for the weekend with a man was a lot more personal than making up her mind whether to become a large-animal veterinarian or which college to attend.

Deciding that she'd have to explain her absence if she did accept Russ's invitation, she took a deep breath. "Uncle Grant, have you met Russ Gannon, the vineyard foreman?"

"No, but I've heard a lot of good things about him." He took a sip of his coffee. "Cole speaks very highly of him. And Eli thinks if Gannon set his mind to it, he could grow grapes on the moon."

"I don't know much about his ability to manage a vineyard, but he is nice," she murmured, wondering how to proceed. This was one of the rare times Abby missed not having a mother or older sister to talk to.

Uncle Grant's green eyes twinkled mischievously. "It sounds to me like he's made quite an impression on you, Sprite."

That's an understatement, she thought, rising to refill their coffee mugs. "Russ took me horseback riding a few days ago and we had dinner at his place last night." When she returned to the table, she met her uncle's curious gaze head on. "And he's asked me to go with him to a rodeo he's competing in down in Wild Horse Flats this weekend."

"Are you going?" Uncle Grant asked, raising one dark eyebrow as he lifted his cup to take a sip.

Abby shrugged. "I'm not sure."

Slowly setting the mug back on the table, he reached across to cover her hand with his. "Are you asking me what I think you should do?"

She frowned. Was she asking for his opinion?

"Not really," she said, thinking aloud. "I just wanted to let you know so that you don't worry if I'm not around this weekend."

"So you're considering it?"

"Yes."

"And you're leaning in that direction?"

When she nodded, he stared at her for several long moments before he finally spoke. "You might not have asked for my opinion, but I'm going to give it to you anyway."

Abby had expected no less of him. "I'm listening."

"You've always been more like a daughter to me than a niece," he said, his voice slightly rough. "And the father in me says hell, no, there isn't a man alive that's good enough for you." He paused to clear his throat. "But you're old enough to know what you want. And you've always had a good head on your shoulders." He gave her hand a gentle squeeze. "I trust your judgment, Abby." He stood up to leave for his meeting. "No matter what choice you make, I know it will be the right one for you."

Rising to her feet, she hugged him. "Thank you, Uncle Grant."

"You're welcome, Sprite." He chuckled as he wrapped her in a bear hug. "Even if I'm not sure what for."

Abby kissed his lean cheek. "For always knowing exactly what to say."

On Thursday afternoon, Russ had just finished grooming Dancer and started brushing down Blue when Abby walked into the stable. He hadn't seen her since driving her back to the carriage house the night he'd had her over for dinner. And, truth to tell, he wasn't the least bit surprised that she'd been avoiding him.

In the past three days, he'd decided that she probably thought he had mush for brains. And he couldn't say he blamed her. They barely knew each other, had been on one date—if that's what dinner at his place could be called—and he'd asked her to go away for the weekend. He knew how much she worried about turning out like her mother. What the hell had he been thinking?

"Hi," she said, walking up to stand on the other side of Blue.

Her soft voice sent a shock wave straight through him, and he gripped the brush he held so tightly, he'd probably end up leaving his fingerprints in the wood.

Damn, but she looked good. Her cinnamon-colored hair was pulled back in a loose ponytail, exposing her slender neck and the satiny skin that he'd love to kiss. His body tightened predictably.

"Hi, yourself," he finally managed to get out around the cotton coating his throat. "I haven't seen you for a while."

"Mercedes asked me to go with her to San Francisco for a couple of days of shopping." She smiled. "I don't think I could have gotten a better workout on a StairMaster."

Laughing, he nodded. "Some of those hills are pretty steep."

They both fell silent, and he knew his invitation was the reason neither of them had much to say. Continuing to brush the gelding, he tried to think of a way to gracefully retract his request before she had the uncomfortable task of turning him down.

When he finally decided to just tell her straight out that he understood why she wouldn't be going with him to Wild Horse Flats, they both spoke at once.

"Abby, I think—"

"Russ, I've decided—"

Stopping, they both laughed nervously.

"Ladies first."

Her gaze dropped to her boot tops and he figured he knew what was coming. But when she raised her gaze to meet his, she smiled. "I've given it a lot of thought and if you still want me to attend the rodeo with you this weekend, I'd like to go."

His heart thumped double-time and he suddenly found it extremely hard to breathe. He'd mentioned the living quarters in the horse trailer having two beds, and he fully intended for her to sleep in one and him in the other. But considering they couldn't keep their hands off each other, she had to know there was a strong possibility they'd end up making love.

The thought had him harder than hell in less than two seconds flat. Resting his forearms on Blue's back, he was glad the gelding stood between them. At least she couldn't see how her accepting his offer affected him, beyond his grinning like a damned fool.

"That's great. Do you think you could be ready to leave by noon tomorrow?" he asked.

She nodded. "When is your first event?"

"Not until Saturday morning. But it's a seven hour drive and I'd like to get there in time to get a good night's sleep."

"I can understand that," she said, running her hand along Blue's back. The horse's hide quivered with pleasure at her touch, and Russ couldn't help but wish it was his skin she was stroking. "Do you want me to come down here early enough to help load the horses?"

"Thanks, but Dancer is the only one I'm taking," he said, laying aside the brush he'd been using on Blue. "A couple of friends called this week and asked me to haze for them during the steer wrestling."

"Okay." She turned to leave. "I guess I'll see you at noon tomorrow."

"Where do you think you're going?" he asked, walking around the roan.

Stopping, she looked uncertain. "I thought I'd go back to the carriage house to start packing."

He shook his head and reached for her. "Don't think you're getting away that easy." Pulling her to him, Russ smiled. "I missed you, Abby."

"I missed you, too."

Her smile sent his blood pressure soaring and, even if his life depended on it, there was no way he could stop himself from covering her mouth with his. The moment he touched her perfect lips, they parted on a soft sigh, and he didn't think twice about slipping his tongue inside.

In the past three days, he'd craved the taste of her, the feel of her body pressed to his. As short a time as they'd known each other, it was completely insane, but he was quickly becoming addicted to her sweetness.

When she responded to his kiss by touching her tongue to his, fire streaked through his veins, and his knees threatened to buckle. He wanted her with a fierceness that robbed him of all reason and, needing to touch her, he slid his palm up along her side to the swell of her breast. He heard her soft intake of breath when he cupped the soft mound with his palm, but to his satisfaction, she didn't pull away. Instead, he felt her arms tighten around him and her fingers grip the back of his shirt for support.

Encouraged by her acceptance of his exploration, he used the pad of his thumb to chafe the hardened tip through the layers of her T-shirt and bra. Her moan of pleasure sent a jolt of desire straight up his spine and caused an answering groan to rumble up from deep in his chest.

Realizing that he was close to losing the tight grip he held on his control, Russ slowly moved his hand down to her waist as he broke the kiss. "Honey, I'd like nothing better than to stay here like this for the rest of the day, but it could prove dangerous."

"Why…do you…say that?" she asked, sounding as out of breath as he felt.

His chest tightened when he leaned back to look down at her. Her porcelain cheeks wore the rosy blush of desire, and her lips were slightly swollen from his kiss. She was absolutely beautiful, and his body throbbed with the need to claim her as his.

He laughed, dispelling some—but not nearly enough—of his pent-up tension. "If this goes on much longer, I'm afraid I might end up suffering the same fate as poor old Harold."

To his surprise, instead of laughing, she shook her head. "You don't need to worry about that ever happening," she said softly. Then, leaning forward, she pressed a kiss to the skin exposed at the open collar of his shirt. "I'll see you tomorrow, Russ."

Feeling as if his heart was about to pound a hole right through his rib cage, he watched Abby walk to the end of the stable and disappear through the wide double doors. He had to concentrate on taking first one deep breath, then another.

He'd bet everything he owned that one of two things was going to happen this weekend. They were either going to make love, or he was going to go stark raving mad.

Five

While Russ parked the gooseneck trailer at the campground next to the rodeo grounds, Abby led Dancer over to the small barn not far from their campsite. When they'd first arrived, Russ had explained that, because of the many small rodeos and horse shows the arena hosted, the campground owners provided stalls for horses as a courtesy to visiting contestants.

After she got the gelding settled into one of the large stalls, she returned to the trailer to find Russ unlocking the door to the living quarters. Grinning, he stepped back and swept off his Resistol in a gallant gesture. "Your home away from home awaits."

Laughing, she stepped up into the camper area of the trailer and looked around. There was a tiny bathroom with a shower, a galley kitchenette and a bench-type sofa that could be converted into a bed. In the elevated gooseneck section, a large, comfortable-looking bed spanned the entire width of the trailer.

"This is really nice, Russ."

He shrugged, but she could tell by the look on his face that her comment pleased him. "It's not The Vines, but it makes traveling a lot easier." He opened the small refrigerator. "Would you like something to drink before we turn in?"

His mention of them going to bed caused her stomach to flutter. They wouldn't be sleeping in the same bed, but there would only be a few feet and a flimsy privacy curtain separating them. Why hadn't she thought of how intimate sharing such a small space was going to be?

Taking a deep breath, she decided it was better not to think of that now. "Thank you, but I think I'll pass on the soda." They'd stopped a couple of hours ago to unload Dancer in order for him to stretch his legs, and, before getting back on the interstate, they'd gotten a burger and French fries at a fast-food restaurant. "I'm still stuffed from dinner."

"I don't see how," he said, frowning. "You ended up giving me most of your fries and part of your sandwich."

"I wasn't very hungry." Abby wasn't about to tell

Russ that her lack of appetite had been due to the butterflies in her stomach that seemed to multiply the closer
they got to the campground.

Switching on the built-in television, he smiled and
reached for the doorknob. "Why don't you kick off your
boots and get comfortable while I feed Dancer and see
that he has plenty of water for the night. When I get
back, it'll just about be time to go to bed."

Every time he made a reference to *night, turning in*
or *bed,* her spine tingled and her stomach did a backflip.
"When does the first event start tomorrow morning?"

"Not until ten, but registration starts at seven," he
said, opening the door. "Besides, we'll need to eat
breakfast. And by that time, I'm betting you'll be pretty
hungry."

"Maybe." She doubted she'd be able to eat much of
anything all weekend.

"Make yourself at home while I'm gone." He stepped
down, out of the trailer. "I'll be back in a few minutes."

Abby waited until he'd closed the door before she released the breath she'd been holding. What on earth
had she been thinking when she'd made the decision to
come to the rodeo with him? The living quarters were
miniscule. And hadn't it been proven, time and again,
that they couldn't be close without falling into each
other's arms?

But even as she questioned her reasoning, she knew

the answer. She simply didn't want to be away from him. And that made no sense at all.

They'd only known each other a little less than two weeks. But when she'd gone on the shopping trip with Mercedes, all she'd been able to think about was getting back to The Vines, and Russ.

Removing her boots, she curled up on the couch and blindly stared at the small television. Could she be falling for him? Was it possible to care for someone that much in such a short amount of time?

When she was with him, she had a sense of belonging, of being where she was supposed to be. And when they were apart, all she could think about was how much she missed his deep laughter, his warm embrace and the kisses that threatened to turn her into a cinder.

Uncle Grant had always said that when she saw something she wanted, she knew it right away and wasn't afraid to go after it. But he'd been talking about her education and career, not affairs of the heart.

Was it time to release the tight grip she'd always kept on herself? Did she dare let herself go, and take the chance that she might fall in love with Russ?

Before she could reach any conclusions about herself and her feelings for Russ, the door opened and he entered the trailer.

"How would you like to go to a dance tomorrow night, honey?"

"Is that part of the rodeo festivities?"

"Not usually." He grinned as he sat beside her on the couch to pull off his boots. "I was talking to a friend of mine down at the barn and he said some of the guys' wives and girlfriends have been complaining about it being Valentine's weekend and them being stuck here at the rodeo."

She laughed. "In other words, the men are trying to make amends by throwing an impromptu dance."

"Something like that. A couple of guys heard their names used in conjunction with 'insensitive' and 'unromantic.' But when some of the women threatened to make them sleep in the barn with the horses, they figured the situation was getting serious." Grinning, he stood to remove his keys and change from his jeans pocket. "So, would you like to go?"

"Sure." She laughed. "It sounds like a lot of fun. But I think I'd better warn you—I haven't gone dancing in ages. I might step on your toes a lot."

His deep laughter sent a tiny electric charge skipping over every nerve in her body. "It won't be a problem. I only dance the slow ones, and mainly just stand in one spot, hold my partner close and sway in time to the music."

The thought of having Russ hold her close made her feel warm all over. Deciding to put a little distance between them, she rose to her feet and looked around for the small overnight bag that she'd given Russ to load into the camper before they'd left The Vines.

"If you could tell me where you put—"

Before she could ask where he'd stored the bag, he reached into the tiny closet and removed some bedding and her overnight case. "Here you go," he said, handing it to her. "The bathroom is pretty small, but I think there's room in there to change."

Stepping into the cramped little room, Abby quickly stripped out of her clothes and put on her nightshirt. But as she started to open the door, she realized that she'd forgotten to pack her robe.

"Now what are you going to do?" she muttered, thoroughly disgusted with herself.

"Did you say something?" Russ called.

"No, just talking to myself."

Glancing down at the thin cotton shirt that ended well above her knees, she decided she had two choices. She could either change back into her clothes and go to bed fully dressed, which wasn't at all appealing. Or, she could hold her head up and act as if nothing was out of the ordinary, walk the few feet to the couch and dive under the covers Russ had taken from the closet.

She really didn't see that she had a choice and before she could chicken out, she opened the door and walked out of the bathroom.

"I could have made my own bed," she said, when she

found him tucking the sheet and blanket under the end of the couch cushion.

"You take the bed. I'll sleep here."

His back was to her, but when he turned around, it was all Russ could do to keep his mouth from dropping wide open. In his entire life he'd never seen a sexier sight than Abby standing there in that light turquoise, oversize T-shirt. It wasn't, by any stretch of the imagination, supposed to be provocative. But he'd never seen her look so hot.

The soft fabric loosely draped her breasts, but did little to hide their hardened peaks, leaving no doubt that she'd removed her bra. When he noticed that the hem of the damned thing barely reached midthigh, it was all he could do to keep from groaning aloud. She had the longest, shapeliest legs he'd ever seen. His overactive imagination—not to mention his hormones—were off and running. When he thought of how it would feel to have her wrapped around him as they made love, his body came to full erection, and he clenched his back teeth together so hard, it would probably take a crowbar to pry them apart.

As he continued to stare, he noticed that Abby's cheeks had turned a pretty pink and he could tell she was embarrassed. But she held her head high and her gaze never faltered.

"I forgot to bring my robe."

Without thinking twice, he stepped forward and pulled her to him. "Don't get me wrong, honey. I'm not complaining about what you're wearing." He drew some much-needed air into his lungs. "Actually, make that what you're *not* wearing. But you're about to give me a heart attack, and it's getting damned near impossible for me to keep my hands to myself."

Her soft body pressed to his was heaven and hell rolled into one, and he'd have liked nothing more than to strip them both, climb into bed and spend the rest of the night loving her. But she trusted him not to push for more than she was ready to give. And he'd walk through hell before he let her down. The only trouble was, he was damned close to reaching his limit, and he was man enough to admit it.

Knowing that he'd be lost if he so much as kissed her, he nuzzled the satiny skin along the column of her neck. "I'm giving this chivalry thing my best shot, honey. But I'm fighting a losing battle. That's why I think it's time for you to go to bed."

When he released her and stepped back to pull on his boots, she looked confused. "Where are you going?"

Reaching for the door, he stopped long enough to give her a quick kiss. "I'm going to run a few laps around the campground, then I'll find a couple of horses to bench-press. After that, I may wrestle a bull or two."

Russ stepped out of the trailer, closed the door behind him and walked away before he could change his mind, go back inside and make love to her until they both passed out from exhaustion.

As he walked down the path to the barn, he released a frustrated breath and willed himself to relax. He was in a place he'd never been before and he had no idea how he was going to handle it, or even if it could be handled. Something told him that it was beyond his control, and that's what had him tied in knots.

There was no doubt that Abby aroused him physically. Hell, he'd been hard almost from the minute he'd laid eyes on her. But the fact that she turned him on emotionally was what had him waging an internal battle with himself.

He'd thought they could have a good time while she was visiting California and, when the time came for her to go back to her farm in Nebraska, there would be no feelings involved and no regrets. But somehow she'd managed to get under his skin as no other woman ever had, and if they made love, he had a feeling he'd never be the same again.

Shaking his head, he sat on a bale of straw outside of Dancer's stall. Something else that had to be considered was the fact that he was almost positive she was still a virgin. And that put a whole different spin on the situation.

He was old-fashioned enough to believe that when

a man took a woman's virginity it meant something more than just a roll in the hay for physical relief. A woman's first time making love should be special, and with a man she cared for deeply and who cared for her in return.

There was no doubt in his mind that they both had that going for them. But the logistics were all wrong for them to build any kind of lasting relationship. Her home was a thousand miles away, and he had nothing to offer her if she stayed here.

Rising to his feet, he slowly started back toward the trailer. If they made love, could they both come away from their time together without suffering some kind of emotional pain? Or when the time came for her to return to Nebraska, would he be able to watch her go without his heart going with her?

The following afternoon, Abby watched Russ back the bay gelding into the hazer's box for the fourth time as he prepared to help another one of his friends compete in the steer wrestling event. He and Dancer were apparently in high demand for the job of keeping the animal on a straight course while the competing cowboy slid from his mount to wrestle the steer to the ground. And Abby knew why. Moving as one, Russ and Dancer made the task look effortless and the cowboys they hazed for did well in the timed event.

"And just where have you been hiding all my life, sugar?" a male voice whispered close to her ear.

Glancing up, Abby found a handsome cowboy with a leering grin preparing to sit down beside her. She scooted over to put as much space between them as possible.

"You sure are a pretty little gal," he said, sitting a bit closer than she was comfortable with.

She'd encountered his type before and giving him a quelling look, she turned her attention back to the action in the arena without comment.

"What's the matter, sugar? Cat got your tongue?" he asked, putting his arm around her.

Without a word, Abby slapped his arm from her shoulders and stood up to find another seat.

"Now that's no way to be," he said, rising to his feet. "I'm just trying to be friendly."

"Number one, I don't want to be your friend," she said, spotting an empty seat several rows down the bleachers. "And number two, my name *isn't* sugar."

He caught her by the arm. "How can we get to know each other if—"

She glared at him as she pulled from his grasp. "If you don't want your hand broken, you'd better keep it to yourself."

Noticing that the steer wrestling event had concluded, she descended the steps and started walking toward the bucking chutes. She spotted Dancer standing docilely just outside the arena gate. But when she looked for Russ, he was nowhere in sight.

"You sure are a feisty little thing," the irritating cowboy said, trotting to keep up with her.

She kept on walking as flashes of the past and a persistent boy named Harold crept into her mind. She tried to quell the sudden twinge of panic that began clawing at her insides. She was longer a teenager and they were far from being alone in a crowd of fifteen hundred people.

"What do you say we find a nice quiet place where we can get to know each other better?" The man slipped his arm around her waist and turned her to face him. "I'd make sure you enjoyed—"

Before she could raise her knee and stop the harassment once and for all, Russ seemed to come out of nowhere to spin the guy around. "Touch her one more time, you son of a bitch, and you'll be picking your teeth out of the dirt."

The man looked as if he wanted to argue the point.

"Go ahead, give me a reason." It was clear that Russ was furious and meant every word he said.

"You're welcome to her, buddy," the cowboy said sullenly as he backed away. "She's not worth that much trouble."

Once the man disappeared in the crowd, Russ turned back to her. "Are you all right?"

She nodded. "I could have handled the situation."

"Not as long as I'm around you won't," he said, taking her into his arms. "You have my word that I'll move heaven and earth to keep creeps like that away from you, Abby."

"I was just about to give him the same lesson in manners that I gave Harold," she said, snuggling into his embrace.

Russ's arms tightened around her. "When I looked up into the stands and saw that bastard's filthy hands on you, I couldn't get off Dancer fast enough."

"Nothing happened." His protectiveness caused a warm feeling to fill every fiber of her being and for the first time in her life, she felt as safe as if she'd been with her uncle, brother, or their hired hand, Buck.

"Honey, I could stay here with you in my arms for the rest of the day, but the bull riding is about to start," Russ said when the next event was announced over the loud speaker. He kissed he temple. "Will you be all right for a few minutes while I go kick some bovine butt?"

Abby raised up on tiptoe to place a kiss on his lean cheek. "I'll be fine, but I want you to promise me something."

"What's that?"

"Be careful."

"You bet." His tender smile sent shivers racing straight through her. "I have a date tonight that I don't intend to miss."

* * *

Two hours later, Abby led the bay gelding back to the barn at the campground and couldn't help but wonder what was going on. Russ had been acting strangely since the conclusion of the bullriding event and immediately afterward, he'd told her he had something he needed to take care of and asked if she minded getting Dancer settled into his stall for the night. Then, handing her his keys to the trailer, he'd given her a quick kiss, got into a truck with another cowboy and left the rodeo grounds in a cloud of dust.

"Your owner is up to something," she told the gelding as she brushed him down. "He has a great ride on an ornery bull, makes the eight-second whistle, then takes off for parts unknown, leaving me and you to fend for ourselves."

Dancer snorted and stomped his foot.

"I couldn't agree more," she said, laughing as she patted his dark brown neck.

Making sure the horse had a fresh bucket of water and a scoop of oats, Abby walked up the path to the trailer. She'd just started to unlock the door to the living quarters when the truck Russ had left in came to a sliding halt a few feet away.

When he got out, he waited until the truck drove on down to a horse trailer several yards away. Then, holding his arm behind him, he walked toward her.

"Did you take care of whatever you needed to do?" she asked.

"Sure did." His smile made her insides quiver when he brought his arm from behind his back and handed her a single red rose in a cut-crystal vase. "Happy Valentine's Day, honey."

Touched by his thoughtfulness, her eyes filled with tears and her hand shook when she took the rose from him. "Oh, Russ! It's beautiful!"

Putting his arms around her, he held her close. "I didn't mean to make you cry."

"I can't help it." She rested her cheek against his wide chest. "This is one of the nicest things anyone has ever done for me. Thank you."

"These are happy tears. Right?"

She nodded. "Oh, yes."

His chest expanded and she knew he was breathing a sigh of relief. "I wanted to buy a dozen, but the florist was closing for the day when J.B. and I got there. We bought the last two roses she had left."

"This is perfect," she said, meaning it.

"I'm glad you like it." He kissed the top of her head. "Now, let's go inside so I can take a shower and change clothes before we go out to dinner and the dance."

"Where's the dance being held?" Abby asked as they left the steak house where they'd had dinner.

When they'd arrived, Russ had said something to the hostess, who'd smiled and led them to a cozy, candlelit table in a corner of the crowded restaurant. On their way to the table, they'd passed a couple of Russ's friends with their dates. But other than polite greetings, the couples, as if by unspoken agreement, had stayed to themselves, and Abby decided it was probably because of the romantic holiday they were all celebrating.

"Some of the guys tried to get a private room at one of the restaurants, but everything was already booked up. That's why we're having the dance at the camp-ground activity center," Russ said, helping her into the passenger side of his truck. "The owner is going to fold the divider back and open up the two rooms for us." He chuckled. "Otherwise, we'd be dancing between the pool and Ping-Pong tables."

She grinned. "I'll feel right at home."

He frowned. "You're kidding."

"No."

He shut the door, then rounded the front of the truck to slide in behind the steering wheel. "How big is Crawley?"

"You should be asking how little it is," she said, laughing. "It only has a population of between five and six hundred."

"That's all?" He looked surprised as he drove out of the restaurant parking lot. "I know you said you came from a small town, but I didn't realize you meant *that* small."

"That's all of the people." She grinned. "But the cattle population is a different story. I think the last survey report from the Ag Department listed about five thousand head of cattle on the farms and ranches surrounding Crawley."

"It sounds like it would have to have a lot of wide-open spaces," he said as he drove the short distance to the campground.

"You'll have to visit sometime and I'll show you around," she said, before she could stop herself.

When he parked the truck beside his trailer, Russ turned and gave her a smile that curled her toes inside her Tony Lamas. "One of these days, I'm going to take you up on that offer."

"Do you mean it?"

She knew she sounded pathetically hopeful, but she didn't care. Despite what she'd told Mercedes about not having time for a man in her life or a long-distance relationship, she couldn't bear the idea of never seeing Russ again.

He gave her a quick kiss, then, grinning, reached for the driver's side door handle. "I have a feeling I'm going to be logging a lot of frequent-flyer miles in the near future, honey."

Abby's heart skipped several beats, and she couldn't believe how relieved she felt knowing Russ wanted them to continue seeing each other after she returned home. When he opened the passenger door, she got out of the truck and wrapped her arms around his shoulders. "I'm going to hold you to that, cowboy."

"I'd rather you hold me against *you,*" he said, pulling her to him. He kissed her until they both gasped for breath, then, stepping back, took her hand in his. "I think we'd better walk over to the dance before I forget I'm supposed to be a gentleman."

She could tell the toll that all of their recent togetherness was taking on Russ. And, for that matter, the weekend hadn't been all that easy for her, either.

When she'd come to California to see why her uncle Grant had extended his stay, she hadn't counted on finding someone special. But from the moment she met Russ, something inside of her—something she hadn't even known existed—had come to life. In his arms, she felt confident and in control, and with his help, she'd realized that she was nothing like her mother.

Glancing up at his handsome face as they walked toward the building where the dance was being held, she knew beyond a shadow of doubt that her first instincts about him had been right on the money. Russ Gannon was trustworthy and honorable and the only man she'd ever met who came close to having the unwavering integrity she so admired in her uncle Grant.

"Hey, Russ!" A cowboy wearing a black Resistol

with a hawk's feather in the hat band waved to them from a table on the far side of the room.

Russ acknowledged the man with a nod of his head as he guided her toward the table. "There's J. B. Gardner. He said he and his wife, Nina, would save us a couple of seats."

As they walked toward the couple, Abby recognized the petite blonde as one of the women she'd seen sitting in the stands of the arena during the day's events.

"I'd just about given up on you, Russ," J.B. said, standing up when they approached.

Making the introductions, Russ held her chair while Abby seated herself at the table. Then, leaning close, he asked, "What would you like to drink, honey?"

A shiver of need streaked through her at the feel of his warm breath on her sensitive skin. "Cola will be fine."

Watching Russ and J.B. walk toward the makeshift bar someone had set up on the other side of the room, Abby couldn't help but smile. He might make wine for a living, but Russ was a cowboy through and through. His shoulders were wide, his hips narrow. But it was his cowboy swagger that made her heart skip a beat and caused a hitch in her breathing.

"I see you like watching Russ as much as I love watching J.B.," Nina said, smiling.

Abby nodded. "It is a nice view, isn't it?"

Laughing, both women looked at each other for a

moment before Nina spoke again. "Do you know how many women's hearts you've broken here tonight?"

Thoroughly confused by her statement, Abby frowned. "I don't understand."

Nina pointed to several women around the room. "See how they're all watching Russ?"

Looking around the room, Abby noticed several women's gazes following him.

When she nodded, Nina went on. "They've had their sights set on Russ for years, but he never seemed to notice." She smiled. "You're the first woman he's ever brought with him to a rodeo."

"Really?" A warmth she couldn't explain coursed through Abby.

"They'd all love to be in your boots right now," Nina said, nodding. Stopping, she grinned. "Or should I say out of them later tonight?"

Abby felt her cheeks grow warm. Before she could think of something to say, the conversation was cut short when someone cranked up the volume on a CD player and several couples walked out onto the improvised dance floor.

"J.B., you big, handsome stud, they're playing our song," Nina said loudly when Russ and the other man walked back over to the table. "What are you gonna do about it?"

"I'm gonna dance with the prettiest gal in the whole

damned state." They set their drinks down, and J.B. grinned as he took Nina's hand and pulled her to her feet. "Come on, baby. Let's see how many times I step on your toes."

Abby couldn't help but smile as she watched the couple move around the dance floor. It was clear Nina and J.B. adored each other.

"Would you like to dance?" Russ whispered close to her ear. His lips brushed her earlobe, and every cell in her being tingled to life.

Unable to find her voice, she nodded and accepted his hand. As they walked out to join the other couples, Abby was conscious of having several women watching them.

Russ took her into his arms. "Do you know how beautiful you look tonight?"

Startled, she shook her head.

He pulled her close. "All of the single men and half of the married ones are wishing they could be me right now."

Smiling, she shook her head and raised her arms to circle his shoulders. "I was thinking that's the way the women felt about me being with you."

When the song ended and another slow tune began, he asked, "Do you want to sit down or dance some more?"

Abby stared up into his handsome face. She loved the feel of his strong arms around her, his hard body pressed to hers. "I think I'd like to dance."

He drew her even closer, and as they moved in time to the music, she felt as if everyone in the room had disappeared. She no longer noticed the envious female stares following their every move. Nothing else mattered but the man holding her so tenderly against him.

When Russ lowered his head to kiss the hollow below her ear, her heart sped up and a delicious wave of goose bumps shimmered over her. She reveled in the contrast of their bodies and how they fit together so perfectly.

"I could hold you like this all night."

His lips skimming her earlobe caused a searing heat to flow throw her veins. Shivering with a need stronger than anything she'd ever experienced, she tightened her arms around his neck and held on to keep from melting into a puddle at his big, booted feet. But when she felt his strong arousal pressing into her soft lower belly, her knees gave way and she sagged against him.

He caught her to him, and as the lead singer of Alabama crooned about how right it felt to be making love to the woman of his dreams, Abby knew in her heart that's what she wanted with Russ. She wanted to feel the depth of his passion, know the power of his lovemaking.

God help her, but she wanted him in a way that she'd never wanted any other man. She wanted him to make love to her.

Six

Russ reluctantly loosened his arms when he felt Abby start to pull back. Damn! He'd done it again. She had to have felt his rapidly hardening body, and it was no wonder she wanted to get away from him. They couldn't be in the same room without him ending up as horny as a seventeen-year-old boy hiding out in the girls' locker room.

Cursing his lack of control, he took a deep breath and gazed down at the most desirable woman he'd ever known. But instead of the uncertainty he expected to see, passion and hunger darkened her emerald eyes to a beautiful forest green. His heart slammed into his rib cage and his body tightened to an almost painful state.

"Abby?"

Leaning forward, she whispered close to his ear. "Let's go back to your camper, Russ."

"H-honey—" he stopped to clear the rust from his throat "—if we leave here now…"

Her sweet, shy smile robbed him of the ability to breathe as she placed her index finger to his lips. "I know."

"Are you sure?" Was she really telling him she wanted them to make love?

"I've never been more sure of anything in my life," she said, nodding.

The air trapped in his lungs came out in one big *whoosh,* and taking her hand in his, Russ led her back to the table where J.B. and Nina were sitting. "Sorry to cut the evening short, but I think we're going to head back to my trailer."

Grinning, J.B. glanced at Nina, then back at Russ. "We were talking about leaving, too."

Russ nodded as he turned to lead Abby to the door. "I'll see you tomorrow morning."

Outside, he breathed in the crisp February air and hoped that it helped slow the adrenalin pumping through his veins. His recently neglected libido was dictating that he scoop Abby up and run to his trailer as fast as his legs could get them there. But as he put his arm around her shoulders and they silently walked the short distance, he willed himself to slow down and consider what their lovemaking would mean for both of them.

He'd bet every dime he had that this would be her first time. And just knowing that she'd chosen him to be the man she gave her virginity to was enough to send him into complete meltdown. But even though she'd assured him that she knew what she was doing, he had to know that she really wanted to make love with him and hadn't based her decision on the heat of the moment. All things considered, it was completely insane, but he wanted her to need him emotionally as well as physically.

When they reached the door to the living quarters of his horse trailer, Russ stopped to gaze down at her. God, she was the most beautiful creature he'd ever seen, and he couldn't believe what he was about to say. It could very well end what would otherwise be the most exciting and meaningful night of his life. But he had to be certain she knew how much their lovemaking would mean to him.

"Honey, as much as I want this, and as hard as it would be to walk away from you now, I'd rather we didn't make love at all than to have you regret one minute of what we'll be sharing."

The feel of her soft palm as she cupped his cheek sent a flash fire straight to his groin, and to his immense relief, her gaze never wavered. "I know exactly what I want, Russ. And I want you."

Pulling her to him, he buried his face in her herbal-scented hair. "Abby, I want you so damn bad, I can't see straight." Then, kissing her temple, he stepped back and dug his keys from his jeans pocket. "Let's go inside."

His fingers felt clumsy as he hurriedly unlocked the door and turned on the light. But once they were standing inside the living quarters, he took the time to put his hat on the top of the tiny closet, shrug out of his jeans jacket, then help her out of her denim coat. She probably thought he'd lost his mind, but that couldn't be helped. He was doing his damnedest to slow down and get enough blood back into his brain in order to think of what he needed to ask her.

Finally feeling a little more in control, he took her into his arms and held her close. He needed to put to rest, once and for all, the question of her virginity. "I have to ask you something and I want you to be completely honest with me, even if you think it's none of my business."

"Okay," she said, sounding hesitant.

Her warm breath on the exposed skin at his open collar sent a wave of heat straight to his groin, and it took every bit of his concentration to string the words together. "Abby, are you still a virgin?"

He heard her sharp intake of breath a moment before she slowly nodded. "Yes."

His gut twisted. "I was afraid of that."

She leaned back to look up at him. "Does it matter?"

"Oh, yeah. It matters a lot." The vulnerable expression on her pretty face had him hurrying to reassure her. "Don't get me wrong. I'm honored that you've chosen me to be the first man to touch you. But it also means that to make love to you, I might hurt you." He ran his index finger along the satiny skin of her jaw. "And I'd rather die than cause you pain in any way."

Her cheeks turned a pretty shade of pink. "I know that I might not enjoy our first time together as much as I will other times," she said, her voice little more than a whisper. "But why did you want to know?"

"Because now that I know you've never made love before, I'm going to take things slower and easier than I might have otherwise." He hugged her close. "I give you my word, Abby. I'll do everything in my power to keep your discomfort to a minimum."

A shiver of excitement coursed through Abby at the heated look in Russ's dark blue eyes as he lowered his mouth to hers. The contact was so gentle, it brought tears to her eyes, and she knew he'd make sure their lovemaking was just as tender and sweet. Any lingering doubts she might have had about her decision to give herself to him evaporated like mist on the wind.

Her eyes drifted shut when he deepened the kiss, and as his tongue stroked hers with the promise of a more intimate union, she felt as if a thousand butterflies had been released inside of her. His hand sliding from her back to lift the hem of her T-shirt caused her heart to skip several beats, and curling her fingers in the fabric of his shirt, she clung to him for dear life.

His calloused hand caressed her skin as he moved it up her ribs to the underside of her breast, and a pulse of need like nothing she'd ever experienced thrummed through her veins. Heaven help her, she wanted to feel his hands on her body, wanted him to touch her in ways no man ever had. But when he released the front clasp of her bra, then pushed the lace aside so he could take the weight of her in his palm, Abby thought she would surely burn to a cinder as waves of heat washed over her.

When her knees failed completely, he caught her to him. "Does that feel good, honey?"

"Mmm."

He grazed her hardened nipple with the pad of his thumb, and she felt as if her soul caught fire. "Why don't we get rid of some of these clothes so I can make you feel even better?" he asked.

When she opened her eyes and met his blue gaze, she realized he wasn't just asking to remove her clothing. He was asking for her trust. Unable to find her voice, she simply nodded and brought her own hands up to the top snap on the front of his shirt.

"Let's do this together," he said, removing his hand from her breast. "I'll take off our boots, then you can remove my shirt."

As he led her over to the couch to remove her boots

and socks, then his, she realized he was setting a slow pace, allowing her to feel comfortable with each step of their lovemaking before they moved on. Emotion filled her at the care he was taking.

When he straightened, he reached for her and pulled her up to stand in front of him. "Your turn," he said, bringing her hands to the lapel of his shirt.

Abby knew Russ was trying to help her feel less vulnerable by having her remove his shirt first. Touched beyond words, she placed a kiss at the top of his exposed collar and delighted in his sharp intake of breath and the darkening of his blue eyes to navy.

Encouraged by his obvious pleasure, she tugged his shirt free from the waistband of his jeans and set to work on the snap closures. She'd never removed a man's shirt before and she found the experience both exciting and empowering.

But when she released the last gripper and pushed the shirt from his wide shoulders, her own breath caught as she reached out to touch the well-defined sinew of his broad chest with trembling fingers. He stood completely still and let her test the thick pads of his pectoral muscles, then outline the ripples covering his flat stomach.

A sprinkling of light brown hair covered his warm skin, then narrowed just below his navel. Unable to stop herself, she traced the thin line until it disappeared beneath the waistband of his low-slung jeans.

Glancing up, she noticed that Russ's eyes were closed, his head thrown back. She was driving him wild, but he was allowing her the freedom to explore his body without interference. Emotion welled up inside of her at his sacrifice.

"Russ?"

"What, honey?" His chest rose and fell with his labored breathing.

Before she lost her nerve, she took his hands and placed them at her waist. "Take off my shirt."

His head snapped forward at the same time he opened his eyes, and, holding her captive with his heated gaze, he did as she requested. Dropping it to the floor where she'd tossed his shirt, he reached up with both hands to slide his fingers under the straps of her bra. Her heart raced, and she wasn't sure that her knees would support her when he slowly slid his palms down her arms, taking the scrap of lace with them.

"You're so beautiful," he said when he cupped her breasts.

He teased the hardened tips with his thumbs, then dipped his head to capture first one nipple, then the other, with his mouth. Abby thought she would surely die from the intense sensations his teasing created, and she had to brace her hands on his biceps for support.

When he lifted his head, he took her into his arms, and the feel of the downy hair covering his chest as it brushed the sensitive tips of her breasts sent ribbons of desire swirling throughout her entire being. Feeling as if warm honey had replaced the blood in her veins, she shivered with a need stronger than she could have imagined possible.

"You feel so damned good, I think I'm going to go off like a Roman candle," Russ said, his voice sounding like a rusty hinge. Setting her away from him, he guided her hands to the button at the top of his jeans. "I don't want to rush you. But if we don't get these off, I'm going to end up hurting something."

Her heart pounded as she pushed the button through the buttonhole, then reached for the metal tab. But when she noticed his arousal pushing insistently against the fly, she shook her head. "I think you'd better do this. I don't want to be responsible for causing you any injury, either."

He glanced down, then, chuckling, he nodded. "You might be right. Zippers and erections can be a dangerous combination."

She watched him carefully ease the metal tab downward, then push his jeans and briefs from his lean hips and down his muscular legs. When he kicked them aside and turned to face her, Abby's heart stopped completely, then took off at a gallop. Russ's body was a work of art—a thoroughly aroused work of art.

The muscles of his wide shoulders, chest and thighs

were well-defined from years of physical labor in the vineyards. His flanks were lean and sleek. But is was the sight of his proud, full erection that sent her pulse racing.

Her gaze flew to his, and his sexy smile caused her insides to quiver and the butterflies in her stomach to flap wildly. She said the first thing that came to mind. "My goodness! That's awfully large."

"Don't be afraid of me." His grin did strange things to her insides when he stepped forward and ran his finger along the top of her waistband. "I'm just a man like any other."

Somehow she doubted that was the case, but the feel of his fingertip brushing the sensitive skin of her belly robbed her of the ability to speak, breathe or even think. She tingled where he touched her, and when he silently asked her with his eyes to take the next step, all she could do was nod.

Russ's heated gaze held hers captive as he released the button at the top of her jeans, then slid the zipper all the way down. Clutching his shoulders for support, she closed her eyes and held her breath when he slowly pushed her jeans down her thighs. She felt him kneel in front of her to lift first one of her legs, then the other, to remove the jeans completely.

With her eyes still closed, she waited for him to do the same with her panties. But when he placed his warm hands on her knees, then slowly skimmed them upward, her body began to tremble with need. His hands stopped at the tops of her thighs, and she felt his fingers trace the elastic around her legs. She forgot all about what she thought he might do next and focused on how he was making her feel.

Caught up in the excitement of his teasing, it took her a moment to realize what he meant to do when he moved his thumbs and they came to rest on the damp fabric between her legs. Her whole body trembled, and she thought she would surely melt when he lightly chafed the most sensitive spot on her body.

Leaning forward, he kissed the skin below her navel. "Do you like that?"

Unable to find her voice, she nodded.

"Do you want me to stop?"

If he stopped now, she was sure she'd die from wanting. "N-no."

"Are you ready for me to take these off?"

The sound of his rich baritone and the light pressure of his thumbs caused a fresh wave of heat to flow through her. "Y-yes."

When he moved his hands to the elastic waistband and removed the sensible cotton panties, she stepped out of them on wobbly legs. She felt an almost uncontrollable urge to cover herself when he straightened and stepped back to look at her. But the appreciation and raw hunger she saw in Russ's eyes stopped her, and she stood proudly before him.

"You're perfect," he said, taking her into his arms.

Her moan mingled with his groan of pleasure as soft, female skin met with hard, male flesh. Sparks of electric current skipped over every nerve in her body at the contact, and caused the threads of desire swirling inside of her to twine together and form a coil of need deep in the very core of her. He kissed her, letting her taste his passion, and when he finally raised his head, they clung to each other as they gasped for breath.

"I—" he cleared his throat "—think we'd better lay down before we collapse."

Abby nodded. "I doubt that my legs are going to support me much longer."

Stepping back, he nodded toward the big bed in the elevated part of the trailer. "Climb in and I'll turn out the light."

She shook her head and bit her lower lip to keep a nervous giggle from erupting. "Not on your life, cowboy. Turn the light off, then I'll get in bed." At his confused expression, she explained, "Can you imagine how undignified and embarrassing crawling into that bed on all fours would be for me? My bare bottom—"

"Don't go there, honey." Groaning, he closed his eyes and she watched his Adam's apple bob up and down as he swallowed hard. "The problem is, I *can* imagine it, and it's about to send me into orbit." He turned off the light. "Now, will you get into bed?"

"Yes," she said, scrambling up onto the wide mattress.

The interior of the trailer was dark, but not so much that she couldn't see his shadowy figure as he bent to pick up his jeans and remove something from the pocket. Her heart raced and she lay perfectly still when he climbed into bed and reached for her. His hair-roughened flesh made her skin tingle and her insides feel as if they'd been turned to warm butter.

"Are you all right?" he asked, kissing her forehead. "Are you still sure you want me to make love to you?"

She knew he was giving her one last opportunity to call a halt to things, in case her nerves had gotten the best of her and she'd changed her mind. His consideration touched her deeply.

"Russ, the only thing I'm certain of is if you don't make love to me, I'll never forgive you," she whispered.

Thanking the good Lord above that she hadn't had a change of heart, Russ cupped her breast with his hand and lowered his head to take her hardened nipple into his mouth. The taste of her was like ambrosia to him, and he didn't think he could ever get enough of her sweetness.

As he circled the tight peak with his tongue, he slid his hand along her side to the flare of her hip, then down to her knees. Her soft, smooth skin was like satin, and as he brought his calloused palm up along the inside of her thigh, she trembled against him.

"Russ?"

He lifted his head from her breast to kiss his way up to her lips, and at the same time, he touched her damp auburn curls. She went perfectly still.

"It's okay, honey. I'm only going to bring you pleasure and make sure you're ready for me."

Lowering his mouth to cover hers, he kissed her deeply as he parted her feminine folds and gently stroked the tiny sensitive nub hidden there. Her nails dug into his shoulders as her passion rose and her lower body moved in time with his hand.

"Does that feel good, Abby?"

"Y-yes."

"Do you want me to do more?" he asked, continuing to coax her body into readiness.

"P-please, do…something," she gasped. "You're making me crazy."

Whispering close to her ear, he let his breath tease her when he asked, "Do you want me inside of you?"

She shivered against him. "Yes! Please…I need—"

"Just a minute," he said, reaching for the foil packet he'd placed beneath his pillow.

Quickly arranging their protection, he nudged her knees apart with his leg, then positioned himself over her. As he gazed down at her passion-flushed face, he didn't think he'd ever seen a more beautiful sight. His chest swelled with an emotion he didn't dare put a name to as he guided himself to her, then slowly, carefully, eased his body forward and into her moist heat. He watched her eyes widen as he continued to move forward. He could tell from the tightness surrounding him that she was tensing in anticipation of the discomfort they both knew was unavoidable.

His body trembled from the need to thrust into her, to completely make her his. But he fought to maintain what little control he had left.

"I feel so...full," she said softly.

He gave her what he hoped was an encouraging smile. "Just a little more and you'll have all of me."

When he felt her become less tense, he once again eased forward until he met the barrier of her virginity. Taking a deep breath, he gathered her to him and lowered his head to hers.

"I'm sorry, Abby," he whispered, covering her mouth with his at the same time he pushed past the thin veil and sank himself completely within her tight heat.

Her startled gasp vibrated against his lips and he hated himself for the pain he'd caused her. But even as he cursed himself, every male instinct he possessed urged him to complete the act of loving her. Clenching his teeth, he forced himself to remain perfectly still and concentrate on the needs of the woman in his arms.

"Take a deep breath and try to relax," he said, brushing her damp hair from her cheek.

The blood pumping through his veins caused his ears to roar, and Russ wasn't sure how much more he could take. With her body holding his captive, her soft warmth surrounding him like a velvet glove, his own body pulsed involuntarily inside of hers and he had to grit his teeth against the red-hot need.

She opened her eyes, and her lips curved up in a shy smile. "That was an intriguing sensation."

Feeling the pressure around him begin to ease, Russ managed a smile. "That's just one of many interesting feelings."

He kissed her forehead and eased his hips back, then forward, as he watched for any sign that he might be causing her more discomfort. When he saw none, he closed his eyes and fought the surge of heat urging him to complete the act of loving her.

"Russ?"

"What?"

"Please make love to me." Her throaty request sent a wave of desire straight to his groin, and he couldn't have stopped himself if his life depended on it.

Slowly rocking against her, he held her soft body to his and fought for restraint. But when Abby began to move with him, to meet him in the sensual dance of love, he thought he'd go up in a blaze of glory.

But all too soon, he felt her body begin to tighten around his, felt her inner muscles cling to him in an effort to hold him even closer. He knew she was close, and quickening the pace, Russ concentrated on bringing her as much pleasure as he possibly could.

Strengthening his thrusts, he felt her inner muscles quiver around him as her passion overtook her and she gave into the storm. Her moist heat pulsing around him, the bite of her nails scoring his skin as she grasped his shoulders and the sound of her crying his name, added to his own rapidly building climax. Groaning her name, he held her to him as he gave in to the fierce need stiffening his body. Then, surging into her one final time, he shuddered as he rode wave after wave of his own release.

When the last of the tremors passed, he buried his face in her soft auburn hair and tried to draw some much-needed oxygen into his lungs. "Are you all right?"

"Oh, Russ."

Her broken whisper caused him to feel sick inside. Raising his head, cold fear snaked up his spine, and he cursed himself as a low-down, sorry excuse for a man when he saw tears streaming from the corners of her eyes.

"Oh, God, Abby. I swear I tried to be gentle. I didn't mean—"

She placed her fingers to his lips to stop him. "I'm fine, Russ."

"Then why are you crying?" he asked, wiping the moisture from her cheeks.

"That was the most beautiful experience of my life." She gave him a watery smile. "Thank you."

Relief flowed through him as he levered himself to her side, then gathered her to him. "No, honey. Thank you for the most meaningful experience of *my* life."

Yawning, she snuggled against him. "Is it always like that, Russ?"

He rested his cheek against her head and enjoyed the feel of her warm breath on his bare chest. "Only when it's the right man and the right woman."

"Mmm." She yawned again. "You're most definitely the right man."

"And you're the right woman," he said, kissing the top of her head. As he listened to her breathing become shallow, his chest tightened at the realization that he'd never find another woman who felt as right in his arms as Abby.

After she drifted off to sleep, Russ lay awake thinking about what they'd shared. Abby had waited a long time to explore her sexuality, and he was honored and humbled that she'd chosen him to be the first man she shared herself with.

But even as grateful as he felt that she'd trusted him to be the man she gifted with her virginity, he knew that nothing could come of their relationship. His life was at The Vines, working for the people who had opened their home to him when he'd had no one to turn to and nowhere else to go.

Besides, Abby deserved the best, and he had very little to offer her. Hell, he didn't even have his own place. What would a well-educated woman like Abby want with a man who had nothing more than a high-school diploma and a secondary degree from the school of hard knocks?

Her life on a Nebraska farm was one that he could only dream of, and although he'd mentioned visiting her, they both knew that wasn't likely to happen. She would return to Crawley, start her veterinary practice and forget he existed. While he would never, as long as he lived, get over holding perfection, then having to let it go.

Russ released a frustrated breath. Abby would be leaving in another week or so, and even though he'd have a hell of a time getting over her, he couldn't bear the thought of being without her. That's why he was going to spend the rest of their time together storing up as many memories as he could until the day came that he had to let her go.

Seven

"**M**ercedes, you look like your mind is a million miles away," Abby said, walking into the woman's office on the second floor of the Louret Winery.

"Actually, it's only a few miles away," she said, motioning for Abby to have a seat. "So, tell me about the rodeo. Did you enjoy yourself?"

Abby felt her cheeks grow warm. "How did you—"

"I overheard Grant interrogating Eli about Russ."

"He didn't."

Mercedes nodded. "Afraid so."

"Oh, good heavens!" Abby's cheeks heated even

more. How many more of the Ashtons knew about her going away with Russ?

It wasn't that she'd tried to hide her relationship with him. But she preferred to keep some things about herself private.

Before she could find something to say, Mercedes smiled. "Don't worry. Your uncle didn't tell Eli about your going away with Russ this weekend. Grant just asked what kind of man Russ is and what Eli knew about him." Mercedes laughed as she leaned back in her desk chair. "Since Eli thinks the world of Russ, he gave Grant a glowing recommendation."

Abby began to relax a bit. "But that doesn't explain how you knew that I'd gone to Wild Horse Flats with Russ."

"I simply did the math," Mercedes said smugly.

"But I don't see how—"

The woman laughed as she ticked off the points on her fingers. "One man leaving town for the weekend. One woman who seemed extremely interested in that man a few days earlier, going missing that same weekend. Add a concerned uncle's questioning of the man's boss and it adds up."

Shaking her head, Abby couldn't help but laugh. "Did anyone ever tell you that you should get your private investigator's license?"

Mercedes shrugged. "I'm not that good, or I'd be able to figure out a way to get into the estate of the esteemed Spencer Ashton."

"Still no progress in meeting with him?" Abby asked sympathetically.

"No. He won't talk to any of us."

"How long has it been since you've seen your father?"

Mercedes looked thoughtful. "I was four when he divorced Mother to marry his secretary, Lilah. And to tell you the truth, I'm not sure I've seen him more than a few times in the twenty-nine years since."

Abby couldn't help but feel sorry for her California relatives. Spencer had walked away from his second family much the same as he'd done Uncle Grant and Grace. The only difference being, he'd stayed in the same area instead of moving over a thousand miles away. It had to have added to the pain and humiliation he'd caused Caroline and her family over the years.

"Have any of you tried going to the estate, knocking on the door and demanding to know why Spencer won't meet with any of you?" Abby asked, wondering if anyone besides Uncle Grant had tried the direct approach.

Mercedes sighed as she shook her head. "I wouldn't be welcome. His wife would probably have a royal fit if any of us stepped foot on the property."

"How rude! You'd think the lady of 'the big house' would be more sociable," Abby said, grinning.

"You'd think," Mercedes said dryly.

When they both stopped laughing, Abby gave the

woman a sly glance. "Didn't I hear someone say they have a lot of charity functions at 'the big house'?"

"They rent the estate grounds and ballroom for special events like weddings and charity fund-raisers," Mercedes said, nodding.

"Do you have any idea when they'll be having the next event?"

"I read an article in the newspaper just this morning about the local equine welfare society holding their annual fund-raiser there tomorrow evening." Mercedes frowned. "Why do you ask?"

"I'm a large-animal veterinarian, not to mention an avid horse enthusiast. And *I'm* very interested in the humane treatment of animals." Abby couldn't believe what she was about to suggest. She'd never crashed a party in her entire life. "How would you like to attend that event tomorrow evening?"

Mercedes sat forward. "Are you serious?"

"Sure." Abby shrugged. "What's the most they can do? Ask us to leave?"

A sly smile curved Mercedes's lips. "If he's not in San Francisco, Spencer might be there. I could try to reason with him, and maybe we'll be able to avoid a more public confrontation."

"That's right," Abby said, grinning. "Actually, when you stop to think about it, you'll be doing him a favor."

"Craig and I were supposed to have dinner tomorrow

evening, but I'm sure I can persuade him to join us." The woman rolled her eyes. "He's always ready to put on a tux and mingle with the society movers and shakers of Napa Valley."

"And I'll see if Russ would like to attend." She didn't think Russ was the type to enjoy something so formal, but she could try.

"Then it's decided," Mercedes said, reaching for the phone. "I'll call Cole and tell him that I'll be out of the office for the rest of the afternoon and all day tomorrow."

Abby frowned. "The event isn't until tomorrow evening. Why would you—"

"Do you have a cocktail dress?" Mercedes asked, smiling as she pressed the phone's keypad.

Laughing, Abby shook her head. "We're going shopping again, aren't we?"

"Yes. And tomorrow we're going to get our hair and nails done." Mercedes suddenly turned her attention to the phone, and Abby listened to her tell her brother she'd be out for the rest of the day. Then, grabbing her purse, Mercedes rounded the end of the desk to take Abby by the arm. "Let's go. I saw a beautiful emerald dress in one of the boutiques in Napa the other day that would be perfect for you."

As she let Mercedes hurry her along, Abby couldn't help but wonder what on earth she'd gotten herself into. She'd never owned a cocktail dress, let alone worn one. There just weren't that many occasions in Crawley that called for anything more formal than boots, jeans and, depending on the weather, a flannel or cotton shirt.

But so far, her trip to California had been filled with firsts. Why not add wearing a formal dress to meet her grandfather?

Now, all she had to do was convince Russ that he should go with her.

As they sat cuddled together on his couch, watching an old John Wayne movie and eating popcorn, Russ wondered what was running through Abby's pretty little head. She'd been giving him strange glances all evening, and a couple of times she'd even acted like she wanted to say something, then changed her mind.

Deciding to find out what was going on, he hugged her close and kissed the top of her head, then asked, "Honey, is there something you want to talk about?"

"Why do you ask?" she murmured, snuggling against his chest.

With her body pressed to his, he had to concentrate on what she'd said. Her answering his question with a question wasn't a confirmation or a denial, but it was enough to raise the hair on the back of his neck and send a shaft of apprehension up his spine. He picked up the remote and paused the movie.

"What's going on?"

He heard her soft sigh a moment before she sat up straight and met his questioning gaze head-on. "Will you go somewhere with me tomorrow evening?"

If she asked him to, he'd probably follow her over a cliff. But the hesitancy in her voice warned him that he'd better ask for a few more details.

"Where are you going?"

"The Ashton estate."

He wasn't sure what he'd expected her to say, but visiting Spencer Ashton's self-made kingdom wasn't it. He'd heard enough about what was going on with her uncle—the Ashtons at The Vines and their quest to confront Spencer—to know that Abby was asking for heartache if she expected a warm welcome from her ruthless grandfather or his gold-digging wife.

"Why would you want to pay them a visit?"

She shook her head. "I still can't believe I suggested it, but Mercedes, her friend Craig and I are going to crash one of their charity functions."

Every one of Russ's protective instincts came to full alert. He didn't like the idea one damned bit. It spelled disaster with a great big capital *D*.

"Are you sure about doing this, Abby? From what I've heard, Ashton's current wife, Lilah, is just short of hostile when it comes to any of Spencer's kids but hers. And as adorable as I know you are, I doubt she'd view his granddaughter any differently."

Abby shrugged. "She won't even know who I am. And from everything that's been said, I'm not sure any of them will recognize Mercedes."

Russ wasn't so sure. "Honey, they may not run with the same crowd as her kids, but you can bet that Lilah Ashton has made it her business to know who Eli, Cole, Mercedes and Jillian are. If nothing else, to keep them away from her kids."

"You really think she's that jealous?" Abby asked doubtfully.

"Oh, yeah." He put his arm around her slender shoulders. "If Lilah Ashton was any other type of woman, she would have encouraged Ashton to stay in touch with his other family."

Looking thoughtful, Abby nodded. "You're probably right. But Mercedes is hoping to see Spencer and convince him that it would be to everyone's advantage for him to meet with Uncle Grant and his other children. I don't think he could argue that airing the family's dirty laundry in the press would be unpleasant for all concerned."

Russ could well understand why no one wanted it to come to that, but the thought of Abby walking into a situation akin to a lamb entering the lion's den didn't sit well, either. Although rubbing elbows with Napa's high society wasn't his idea of a good time, he didn't like, nor did he trust, Craig Bradford to protect Abby and Mercedes from public humiliation. The man was too slick and impressed with himself.

Russ didn't see that he had any other choice. "Do I need a tux?"

"You'll go?" She looked so happy and pleased that Russ decided it would be well worth dressing up in a monkey suit and feeling like a fish out of water just to see her smile the way she was doing now.

He nodded. "There's no way I'm going to let you go by yourself. What time do I need to pick you up?"

"Oh, Russ, thank you," she said, throwing her arms around his neck.

Her obvious delight in his decision to go with her had him deciding that he'd walk through hellfire itself if that's what she wanted him to do. All she had to do was ask.

She leaned back to give him a smile that sent his blood pressure soaring and his heart thudding against his ribs. "You think I'm adorable?"

Smiling back at her, he nodded. "Absolutely. And I intend to show you just how much."

"That sounds interesting."

The heightened color on her porcelain cheeks told him that she knew exactly what he had in mind. The expression on her beautiful face said she completely agreed with his method of choice.

Her soft body pressed to his and the spark of desire he detected in her pretty, green eyes had him forgetting all about charity functions, or that going to the Ashton estate could prove disastrous. All that mattered was the woman in his arms and how much she made him want her.

Rising to his feet, Russ held out his hand and, to his satisfaction, there wasn't a moment's hesitation when Abby took it. Neither spoke as he led her into his bedroom and closed the door. Words were unnecessary. They both wanted the same thing—to once again share the intimacy they'd discovered over the weekend.

He reached up to remove the pink elastic band holding her auburn hair in a ponytail, then threaded his fingers through the silky strands. He loved the cinnamon color, the smell of her herbal shampoo.

"You should wear your hair down more often," he said, lightly kissing her temple. "It's beautiful."

He started to take her into his arms, but to his delight, Abby had other ideas. Placing both hands on the lapels of his shirt, she gave them a quick tug and the snap closures easily popped free. In no time at all, his shirt was lying in a crumpled heap at his feet.

Amused and more than a little curious to see what she intended to do next, he stood perfectly still, watching her. He didn't have long to wait.

She gave him a smile that sent liquid fire coursing through his veins, and it felt as if he'd been branded by her touch when she placed her soft, warm palms on his chest. She lightly moved her fingers over his skin, and Russ sucked in a sharp breath. But when she circled his flat nipples, then skimmed his puckered flesh with her fingertips, it felt as if an electric charge streaked straight to his groin, and it damned near brought him to his knees.

"Do you like that?" she asked, continuing her exploration of his chest and abdomen.

He nodded. "If it felt any better, I'd think I'd died and gone to heaven."

Her hands drifted lower and her sexy little grin warned him there was more to come. "Could you tell me something?"

"What do you want to know?"

She traced the thin line down from his navel to the top of his jeans. "Why do most men have this, even if they don't have hair on their chests?"

Finding enough air to breathe was becoming more difficult with each passing second, and the ability to think, all but impossible. But when her question registered in his oxygen-deprived brain, he couldn't help but chuckle. "You mean the Paradise Trail?"

Her slumberous smile tightened his body further. "That's not really what it's called, is it?"

"Paradise Trail, Treasure Trail, Straight Line to Heaven—it's known by a variety of names," he said, shrugging.

She laughed, and the sound was one of the sweetest he'd ever heard. "You've got to be kidding. I can't believe the way you guys name everything."

"Nope. I'm not kidding." Giving her a meaningful smile, he took her into his arms and leaned down to whisper close to her ear. "As soon as we get into bed, I intend to give you a refresher course on just how that little line got its name."

"I—I'm going to hold you to that, cowboy." She shivered against him, and the feel of her soft, pink T-shirt brushing his chest reminded him that they had several barriers between them before he could do that.

"Let's get undressed so I can show you."

He caught her gaze with his, and together they silently removed each other's clothes. When the last article dropped to the mingled pile of his and her clothing, he drew her to him. The feel of her warm body against his sent a shock wave all the way to his soul and caused him to harden to an almost-painful state.

Her nipples scored his skin, and he didn't think twice about lowering his head to take one of the tight peaks into his mouth. Pleasuring first one coral peak, then the other, he was rewarded by her moan of delight and the way she had to grasp his biceps for support. He loved giving her pleasure.

But when she arched into his embrace, the feel of his erection pressing into her soft lower belly threatened to buckle his knees and had him wondering how much longer he'd be able to keep them both on their feet. Sweeping her up into his arms, he carried her the short distance to place her in the middle of his king-size bed.

Gazing down at the most beautiful woman he'd ever known, he did his best to commit every detail of the moment to memory. Her silky hair spread across his pillow, the passion in her pretty emerald eyes and the contrast of her porcelain skin against the navy-blue sheets was a sight he knew for certain he'd remember for the rest of his life.

When he stretched out beside her, he took her into his arms and, lowering his head, traced her lips with his tongue. She opened for him and he slipped inside, reveling in the way she moaned and pressed herself to him.

Lost in reacquainting himself with her sweetness, in bringing her to new heights of passion with his kiss, Russ was completely unprepared when she moved her delicate hand down his side, then circled him with her soft palm. Her innocent touch sent a surge of red-hot desire racing through him and robbed him of the ability to breathe.

"H-honey, what—" he had to stop and grit his teeth against the wave of intense pleasure streaking through every cell of his being "—do you think you're doing?"

"I hope I'm making you feel good," she whispered.

The husky sound of her voice and her warm breath

feathering over his skin sent a flash of heat straight to his groin. Russ could no more have stopped himself from moving into her innocent touch than he could stop the ocean waves from crashing onto the shore.

But as she stroked his fevered flesh with her soft palms, then explored the heavy softness below, Russ groaned deeply and reached to take her hands in his. Lifting them to his mouth, he kissed her fingertips and shook his head. "Don't get me wrong. I love what you're doing. But much more of this and I can't be held responsible for what happens."

"Really?"

He nodded as he placed her hands on his shoulders, then pulled her more fully against him. "I plan on being inside of you for the grand finale." He kissed the fluttering pulse at the base of her throat. "And when I go, I fully intend to take you over the edge with me."

"Russ, please make love to me." Her throaty plea sent his blood pressure soaring.

Reaching into the nightstand's drawer, he removed one of the small foil packets he'd placed there earlier and tore it open. But to his surprise, when he started to arrange their protection, Abby took it from him.

"Do you mind if I help?"

Swallowing hard, he shook his head. "Do you know how?"

She nibbled her lower lip as she shook her head. "Not really. But it can't be that hard."

Laughing, he guided her hands to him. "That's the problem. I think I'm harder than I've ever been in my life."

Her cheeks colored a pretty pink. "I didn't mean…"

"I know." Grinning, he gave her a quick kiss, then lay back against the pillows. He'd never had a woman take the initiative to arrange their protection. He found Abby's taking charge immensely exciting. "I'm all yours."

Fascinated by what she intended to do, Russ watched her for several moments as she tried to figure out how to put the condom on him. Smiling, he showed her what to do, and in no time, they had the preventive measure in place.

He turned her to her back, then leaned over to kiss her eyes, her nose and the hollow below her ear. "Now, that wasn't too difficult, was it?"

She shook her head. "It wasn't hard at all."

He chuckled as he moved closer and pressed his arousal to her thigh. "Like I told you before, honey, being hard isn't an issue."

"I, uh, think I understand." Her breathless tone heated his blood further and had his heart racing at about a hundred miles an hour.

Without a word, he moved over her. But when he started to make them one, she gently brushed his hand aside and took charge again. Guiding him to her, her emerald eyes sparkled with a hunger that matched his own need, and as he slowly sank himself in her moist heat, Russ was filled with an emotion deeper and more meaningful than anything he'd ever experienced. If he had let himself think about it, it might have scared him spitless. But with her body wrapped around him like a silken sheath, all of his senses were focused on completing the act of loving her.

Their gazes locked, and as Russ set a slow pace, he watched Abby's expression change as her passion began to build. Her cheeks flushed with the rosy blush of desire, and the hungry fire glowing in her eyes made his heart hammer in his chest. She was sharing more than her body with him. She was sharing her heart, her soul.

All too soon, he felt her body begin to tighten around him and he knew she was close to the peak. His own body responded with the need to empty himself inside her, but he held back. He'd made her a promise—that he intended to take her with him when he found release from the storm—and, reaching between them, he touched her intimately.

Her feminine muscles held him to her, as if she was trying to make him a permanent part of her, a moment before they quivered around him as she found the ecstasy they both sought. Unable to restrain himself any longer, Russ let go of the control he'd fought so hard to maintain. His own muscles contracted, then surged, as he gave up his essence and joined her in the mind-shattering release.

Completely exhausted, he used his last ounce of strength to wrap her in his arms and turn them to their sides. Abby was the most responsive, incredible woman he'd ever known, and there wasn't a doubt in his mind that the feelings filling him at that moment went further than the fulfillment of desire, or a man and woman simply coming together out of mutual need.

His heart hammered at his ribs so hard, he was surprised it wasn't deafening. Could he be falling in love with Abby?

When she snuggled against him and dozed off into a peaceful sleep, Russ hugged her close as he stared at the ceiling and tried to come to grips with what he suspected. What happened to his plan of showing her a good time while she was in Napa, then settling back into his old routine once she returned to Nebraska?

But as he lay with her soft, warm body pressed to his, he shook his head at his own foolishness. He had a feeling that he'd never had a chance. Unless he missed his guess, he'd been a goner from the moment their eyes met that first day in the stable.

Eight

With her hand in Russ's, Abby took a deep breath to steady her nerves as they followed Mercedes and Craig across the Ashton estate's east-wing veranda. Not only was she apprehensive about breaking an ankle in the three-inch heels that Mercedes had insisted she buy, now that they were actually ready to enter the home of Spencer Ashton, Abby was having second thoughts.

What had she gotten them all into? Would Mercedes be treated well? Or would Spencer's wife and children descend on her like a flock of vultures?

Abby wasn't worried about what they would say to her. For one thing, they didn't even know who she was.

And for another, she had never had a problem standing up for herself. She barely suppressed a nervous giggle. If there was any doubt about that, they could always get in touch with poor old Harold. He could verify that she was anything but a pushover.

"Are you doing okay?" Russ asked as they approached the entrance.

Nodding, Abby smiled and leaned over to whisper in his ear. "How could I not be feeling fantastic with you as my date? In jeans and chambray shirt you're very handsome. But in a tux you're downright delicious."

"Honey, I was thinking you're the one who looks delicious." He gave her a wicked grin. "But as good as you look in that green dress, I can't wait to help you out of it later tonight."

A shiver of excitement coursed through her. He knew just what to say to get her mind off what they were all about to do. Was it any wonder that she'd fallen head over heels in love with him?

"I'm looking forward to getting you out of that tux, too," she said, feeling extremely breathless all of a sudden.

As they entered the reception hall, Abby couldn't help but marvel at the opulence of her grandfather's estate. The room was very elegant, with its beige faux-stone walls, heavy silk draperies and highly polished marble floors. It reminded her of a palace.

"This is a far cry from Spencer's Nebraska roots," she murmured.

"It's a far cry from the way we grew up at The Vines," Mercedes said, her tone tinged with bitterness. "By all rights, this place should belong to my mother."

Abby couldn't say she blamed Mercedes for feeling the way she did. After Caroline's father left the Lattimer Corporation to Spencer, he'd used his shrewd business sense, and a few illegal moves, to take control of not only John Lattimer's vast holdings and fortune, but also the family estate—a home that had been in the Lattimer family for years. He'd left poor Caroline and their four children with nothing more than the house and small vineyard that had belonged to her mother's family. He had paid a paltry amount of child support for Eli, Cole, Mercedes and Jillian, but beyond that he'd cut them out of his life completely.

Reaching out, Abby gave Mercedes's hand a gentle squeeze. "My great-grandmother Barnett always said that what goes around comes around. One day, Spencer's dirty dealings will catch up with him and he'll end up being the loser."

Mercedes gave her a grateful smile. "I hope I'm around to see it happen."

"Champagne?" a uniformed waiter asked, walking up to them.

Craig took one of the crystal flutes, filled with pink sparkling wine, from the ornate silver tray the waiter held, then looked around the room as he straightened his bow tie. "You don't mind if I mingle a bit, do you?"

"Go," Mercedes said, rolling her eyes.

"Would either of you like champagne?" Russ asked, reaching for two of the remaining glasses.

Abby smiled and shook her head. "None for me, thank you."

Mercedes smiled as she accepted the glass Russ handed her. "Thank you, Russ." To Abby she added, "At least your date is a gentleman."

"Is Craig always this…" Abby's voice trailed off as she tried to think of a diplomatic way to describe how insensitive the man was.

"Callous? Self-absorbed? Shallow?" Mercedes finished for her. When Abby nodded, the woman shrugged. "I always come in second when Craig has the opportunity to circulate with the social elite of Napa Valley. I guess I'm used to it by now."

Before Abby could ask Mercedes why she continued to see the man, a beautiful young woman with long, ash-blond hair and striking green eyes walked up to them. "Welcome to the Napa Valley Equine Society's annual fund-raiser." She smiled and held out her right hand. "I'm Megan Ashton, the hostess and event planner here at the Ashton estate. If there's anything you need, please don't hesitate to let me know."

The moment of truth had arrived, Abby thought as she shook the woman's hand. She noticed that Russ tensed at her side. He was apparently expecting a confrontation, too.

"I'm Abigail and this is Mercedes."

When the woman offered to shake Mercedes' hand, Abby held her breath. "I'm really pleased you could join us this evening."

"Our last name is Ashton," Mercedes said without preamble. "Abby is your niece from Nebraska and I'm your half sister."

Clearly startled by the revelation, Megan's eyes widened and a quiet gasp escaped her lips. "Oh, my. I've always wondered if we'd meet one day."

Before Abby could assure the woman that they weren't there to cause trouble, a tall, red-haired, middle-aged woman hurried over to them. "What are *you* doing here?" she demanded, pointing a perfectly manicured finger at Mercedes.

"Mother, this is—"

The woman's blue eyes sparkled with anger as she cut Megan off. "I know who she is."

"Hello, Lilah," Mercedes said coolly.

"You have a lot of nerve showing your face around here," Lilah retorted. Her voice held a wealth of anger, and Abby suspected that, though the woman might have all the trappings of wealth and position, happiness with Spencer Ashton had definitely escaped her.

Abby watched Mercedes's chin rise a notch as she met the woman's irate gaze head-on. "I have just as much, if not more, right to be here than you do."

Mercedes hadn't raised her voice much above a whisper, but her meaning couldn't have been clearer if she'd shouted it. She was letting Lilah know that she knew her affair with Spencer all those years ago had been a contributing factor to the breakup of Caroline's marriage to him.

"How dare you come into my house and—"

"Whose house?" Mercedes asked quietly. "This estate belonged to my mother's family long before Spencer married her or you became his secretary."

Abby had to give Mercedes credit for keeping her voice low and remaining calm. But Lilah wasn't quite so diplomatic. She looked as if she might pop a blood vessel at her temple, and drew attention to the fact that she'd obviously had plastic surgery. There was no way a woman her age could get away without having a few crow's-feet around her eyes, unless she'd had some kind of cosmetic procedure.

"Get out!" Lilah screeched. "If you don't leave immediately, I'll—"

"You'll do nothing, Mother," Megan said, placing her

hand on Lilah's arm. She nodded at the group of people that had moved in close, no doubt hoping to hear a juicy piece of gossip they could pass along to their friends. "Please. You're creating a scene."

When Lilah looked around at the gathering crowd, she pasted on the most fake smile Abby had ever seen. "Just a little misunderstanding. Nothing to worry about." With a final glare at Mercedes, she turned and strolled from the room like a queen dismissing her court.

"I'm really sorry for Mother's display," Megan apologized. "She can be…difficult at times."

"Is your father going to be here?" Abby asked.

Megan shook her head. "He rarely attends these events." She smiled sadly. "You were hoping to talk to him, weren't you?"

Mercedes nodded. "I thought maybe…" She stopped and shook her head. "Never mind. It's not important."

"I'm sorry," a uniformed maid said, stopping a couple of steps behind Megan. "Ms. Ashton, you're needed in the kitchen."

"I'll be right there." She gave Abby and Mercedes a smile. "I'll only be a few minutes. Please feel free to look around."

"We really should be going." Mercedes smiled sadly. "I'm sorry if we caused you problems."

"Thank you for being so kind," Abby said, meaning it.

"Don't worry about it." Reaching out to take one of

Mercedes' and Abby's hands in hers, Megan smiled. "I'm glad we finally met."

"Megan?" Mercedes nibbled on her lower lip a moment before she reached out and gave the younger woman a quick hug. "Me, too."

Abby thought Megan's eyes looked suspiciously moist when she nodded, then, turning, disappeared into the crowd.

"I'll go find Craig," Russ said, leaving Abby's side for the first time since their arrival at the estate.

"Well, I guess this was a wasted trip," Mercedes said, sounding tired.

Shaking her head, Abby looped her arm with Mercedes'. "I think it turned out to be quite nice. You discovered that Spencer's other Napa Valley offspring aren't all that hostile, even if their mother is."

Mercedes looked thoughtful. "Megan was quite nice, wasn't she?"

"Yes, she was." Wanting to lighten the somber mood, Abby grinned. "Lilah, on the other hand, was a real piece of work. I wonder what she would have done if I'd thrown my arms around her and called her Grandma."

"I can't believe you said that," Mercedes said, laughing so hard, several people turned to see what was so humorous. "You are *so* bad."

"I know. But don't you think it would have been interesting?"

"Right up until the paramedics hauled her away, after she had a stroke." Her laughter fading, Mercedes hugged Abby. "Thanks for being here with me. I wouldn't have had the courage to do this without you."

Abby hugged her back. "I just wish Spencer had been here."

"Maybe another time," Mercedes said, looking resigned.

As she watched Russ and Craig cross the room, Abby hoped for all their sakes that there was a next time, and that Spencer came to his senses. Otherwise, all hell was going to break loose when Uncle Grant went to the press with the story of Spencer's transgressions.

Russ focused on Abby as he and Craig walked over to where she and Mercedes stood by the door of the reception hall. He couldn't believe how well she'd handled the situation with Lilah and Megan Ashton. She hadn't said much, but she'd clearly been the quiet strength that had allowed Mercedes to face the Dragon Lady and come out the winner.

His chest swelled with an emotion he didn't dare put a name to. Abby was amazing in so many ways. She could heal an animal's wound with her gentle touch, dress up and circulate among the social elite like she was born to it, and she had more courage in her little finger than most people had in their whole damned body. Was it any wonder that he was close to falling for her?

But as he thought of how special Abby was, he also thought of how little he had to offer her, and of how one day she'd get tired and move on to some guy who was more her equal. She was as comfortable in an evening dress as she was in jeans and boots, while he felt like a fish out of water when he had to get dressed up and hobnob with the social set. She'd graduated from veterinary school with honors, and in record time. He, on the other hand, was still enrolled in the school of hard knocks. What kind of a future could they possibly build together with differences like those?

A sinking feeling chilled him all the way to his soul. If he hadn't realized it before, he sure as hell had it figured out now. He had no other choice but to break things off between them before he got in any deeper. Otherwise, he didn't think he'd be able to survive when the time came to let her go.

"I don't know why we have to leave now, Mercedes," Craig complained. "We only arrived a half hour ago. I was in the process of making several useful contacts."

"I just don't feel like staying any longer," Mercedes answered.

As they walked out onto the veranda and Russ handed the ticket for his truck to one of the parking attendants, he had an almost uncontrollable urge to plant his fist in Craig's nose. Russ never had cared for the man and now he knew why. Besides his blond surfer-boy good looks and slick charm, there was very little to Craig Bradford. He had all the sensitivity, and about as much of the ambition of a damned garden slug.

"Well, just because you're ready to leave doesn't mean that I am," Craig said petulantly.

Russ watched Mercedes rub her temples as she shook her head. "I'm not really up to arguing about this right now, Craig."

Having heard enough, Russ asked, "Will you excuse me and Craig for a minute?"

Abby shot him a questioning look. "Sure."

"Come on, Craig," Russ said, taking the man by the arm. "We have something we need to talk over."

Craig looked apprehensive. "Wh-what's that, Gannon?"

When he was certain the women couldn't hear what he had to say, Russ lowered his voice to a menacing growl. "Shut the hell up about your damned contacts and think about someone besides yourself for a change. If you'd stuck around instead of going off to rub elbows with people who don't give a rat's ass about you or what you're selling this week, you'd know that Mercedes just had a stressful encounter with Spencer Ashton's wife. She doesn't need to listen to your bitching, pal."

"I don't need you telling me—"

"Save it, Bradford," Russ said tightly. "Just show a little compassion."

Before Craig could protest further, Russ walked back to where the women stood. To his satisfaction, Craig returned to Mercedes' side and, although it wasn't the most sensitive of gestures, reached out to take her hand in his. Maybe there was hope for the man after all.

"What was that all about?" Abby asked quietly.

Russ shrugged. "Nothing. Just some guy talk."

When the attendants pulled his truck and Bradford's Beemer to a stop in front of them, Russ helped Abby into the passenger side, then walked around to slide in behind the steering wheel. He forgot all about the other couple when she gave him a smile that sent his blood pressure soaring.

"Are you ready to get out of that tux, cowboy?" she murmured.

As much as he'd like to consider himself an honorable man, Russ knew that tonight he didn't have a choice. He was going to be selfish and make love to her one last time before he had to let her go.

Forcing a smile, he nodded. "I'm not only ready to get out of this monkey suit, I'm ready to get you out of that sexy little green dress."

"Then what are you waiting for?" she asked, her tone so seductive that his heart went into overdrive and the blood in his veins began to heat.

The ride to The Vines was made in relative silence, and as soon as Russ closed the cottage door behind them, he took Abby into his arms. Resting his forehead against hers, he stared down into her luminous green eyes.

"I've wanted to do something all evening," he said, finding it extremely hard to draw his next breath.

Wrapping her arms around his waist, she smiled. "You mean besides taking off my dress?"

Nodding, he reached up to cup her soft cheeks with his hands as he lowered his head. "I've wanted to do this."

He pressed his lips to hers as he once again explored and tasted the most perfect woman he'd ever known. He was determined to commit every detail of this night to memory, to make their loving something neither of them would ever forget. But when he moved to deepen the kiss, Abby had ideas of her own.

When she slipped her tongue inside to stroke and tease his, the flame igniting in his soul threatened to consume him. She was arousing him in ways he'd never believed possible, and he wasn't even sure she realized it.

As her lips moved over his, her hands busily worked at the stud fasteners of his shirt, and in no time at all she pushed the lapels aside to place her palms on his chest.

She broke the kiss, and the smile she gave him caused his heart to stop completely, then start racing at breakneck speed. Her eyes twinkled with mischief and he wondered what she was planning next.

But he ceased thinking altogether when she began to kiss his collarbone, then nibble her way down to the pads of his pectoral muscles. Every touch of her soft lips on his rapidly heating skin sent a tiny charge of electric current shooting straight through him. But when she touched his flat nipple with her lips, then slowly teased it with her tongue, he felt as if he'd been struck by a bolt of lightning.

"H-honey…" His voice sounded like a rusty hinge, and he had to stop to clear his throat. "I'm pretty sure you're going to cause me to have a heart attack."

The sultry look she gave him when she raised her head sent a shaft of desire coursing through every cell in his body. "Do you want me to stop?"

He swallowed hard in an attempt to moisten the cotton coating his throat. "No."

"Good." Smiling, she took his hand and led him toward his bedroom. "I'm feeling a little experimental tonight. Do you mind?"

The suggestive tone in her velvet voice, the look of hunger in her pretty emerald eyes and the images of what she might have in mind sent a shaft of deep need straight to his groin. What man in his right mind would object to a beautiful woman wanting to have her way with him?

"I don't mind at all," he said, struggling to draw some much-needed oxygen into his deprived lungs. "This is starting to get real interesting."

When they were standing beside his bed, he wondered what she intended to do next. He didn't have long to wait to find out when she slid his tuxedo jacket off his shoulders, then unfastened his cuff links and removed his shirt.

Fascinated by every move she made, he sucked in a sharp breath at the feel of her hands touching his belly as she worked the button free at his waistband. But when she eased the tab of his fly down, her slender fingers brushed against the cotton fabric covering his insistent erection, and he had to grit his teeth against the intense sensations tightening his body.

"I'm not sure how much more of this I can take," he said through gritted teeth. Reaching for the zipper at the back of her dress, he smiled. "As good as you look in this little green number, you're going to look better out of it."

He wasn't prepared for her to step back and shake her head. "Not yet, cowboy. You've been exploring my body for the past few days. Now it's my turn to explore yours."

When she smiled and ran her finger down his chest and belly to the waistband at the top of his briefs, his pulse roared in his ears. "I think I've created a monster."

Her smile just about turned him wrong side out. "That's because you're so good at making love to me."

His heart pounded inside his chest like an out-of-control jackhammer. "I think…there's something…you should know." He felt as if he'd run a long-distance marathon. "If you keep touching me and…talking that way, I'm not going…to be able to take much in the way of exploration."

"Really?" She held his gaze with hers as she slowly pushed his slacks down to his knees.

"Not much at all," he said, sounding strangled. He gritted his teeth and desperately tried to slow the fire building in the pit of his belly.

Straightening, she slid her fingers beneath the elastic band of his briefs, then eased the cotton fabric over his arousal and down his thighs. Her touch just about sent him into orbit. But when she took him into her soft, warm hands, he felt as if his head might shoot off his shoulders like a Roman candle.

Abby used her fingers to trace his length and girth while she cupped the softness below with her other palm. The rush of desire that coursed straight to his groin made him light-headed.

He caught her hands in his and placed them on his chest. "Honey, don't get me wrong. What you're doing feels good. Real good. But if you keep that up, in about two seconds flat, I'm going to disappoint both of us."

"I'm making you feel that good?" she asked, looking pleased.

Russ groaned. "If it felt any better, I'd probably set

the house on fire." He finished shucking his slacks and briefs, then, kicking them aside, he reached for her. "Now it's time for a little retaliation."

Her dimples appeared as a slow grin curved her sensuous lips. "What did you have in mind?"

He held her close as he slid the zipper down the length of her back with one hand. "I've been wanting to take this dress off you all evening," he said, kissing the satiny skin along the column of her neck.

Raising his head, he held her gaze with his, placed his hands on her shoulders and brushed the garment down her arms to let it fall into a pool around her feet. But when he noticed what she had on under the Kelly-green silk, his heart stalled and his knees threatened to fold beneath him.

The scraps of satin and lace barely covered her and couldn't, by any stretch of the imagination, be called underwear. Underwear was sensible and made of cotton. What Abby wore was definitely lingerie. And damned sexy lingerie, at that.

"I'm glad I didn't know you were wearing this under your dress," he said, touching the lace garter belt holding up her nylons.

"Why?" The heightened color on her porcelain cheeks, and her breathless tone, told him that she was as turned on as he was.

He grinned as he unhooked the closure at the valley

of her breasts. "I would have spent the entire evening trying to hide the fact that I was hard as hell." Pulling the straps from her shoulders, he tossed the scrap of lace aside, then filled his hands with her. "You're so beautiful," he said, lowering his head to take one coral nipple into his mouth. Running his tongue over the tight peak, he tasted her, then sucked the tight bud until she moaned with pleasure. "Do you like that?"

"Mmm."

"Want me to stop?"

"I'll never forgive you if you do." She traced her fingers over his own puckered flesh. "Does that feel as good to you as it does when you touch me?"

He closed his eyes as a shudder ran the length of him. "Oh, yeah."

Before she could do anything else that threatened to send him over the edge, he removed the garter belt, nylons and the miniscule triangle at the apex of her thighs. Then, pulling back the colorful quilt, he smiled. "Let's get into bed."

Her smile sent his hormones racing. "Okay. But keep in mind, I'm not finished experimenting."

Groaning, he stretched out on the bed. He was so hot and ready for her, he was sure the sweet torture she was putting him through would send him up in a puff of smoke at any moment.

As he watched, she took a foil packet from the bedside table, arranged their protection, then straddled his hips and guided him to her. His blood pressure spiked, and he gripped the sheets with both hands in an attempt to slow himself down as he watched her body take him in. The feel of her melting around him threatened what little restraint he had left.

Breathing deeply, Russ had to remind himself that this was Abby's night, and he refused to take the control away from her. Even if he was suffering from the need to thrust into her until they both reached a soul-shattering climax.

Her eyes sparkled with heated passion as, without a word, she slowly began to rock against him, and he didn't think he'd ever see a more beautiful sight than the woman holding him so intimately. As she moved, her body caressed him and shredded every good intention he possessed.

The white-hot haze of passion surrounding him blinded him to anything but the need to once again make her his. Unable to stop himself, he grasped her hips and held on as she rode him to the point of no return. Never in his entire life had a woman possessed him so fully. At that moment, she owned him, body and soul.

Her moan of pleasure signaled that she was right there with him, and he felt her inner muscles urging him to completely surrender himself to her. Unable to hold back any longer, Russ thrust into her one final time and, groaning, gave himself up to her demands as they became one body, one heart, one soul.

Nine

As Russ stood at the kitchen window watching the darkness of night fade into the pearl-gray light of dawn, he couldn't stop thinking about the incredible night he'd just spent with Abby. She'd loved him with such unbridled abandon that just the thought of it made him hard.

But instead of rejoining her in his bed this morning, as he'd like to do, he was steeling himself to what he knew in his heart was the best for both of them. Last night, he'd purposely put out of his mind the fact that it was their last time together. He hadn't wanted to think about never again hearing her whisper his name as he brought her pleasure, never seeing the blush of satisfaction on her pretty face when she came apart in his arms.

His chest tightened. He'd never felt as complete, as whole, as he felt when he was with her. From the first time he'd held her, he'd felt as if he'd found the other half of himself.

But their being together was something that would, in the end, spell heartbreak for both of them. He wasn't nearly good enough for her, and he didn't think he'd be able to bear the look of disappointment on her pretty face when she finally figured that out. That's why he had to end things now before either of them got in any deeper.

As he stood at the window, staring blindly at the lake behind the cottage, he sensed her presence a moment before her arms circled his waist from behind. The feel of her soft body plastered to his back sent a flash fire zinging through his veins, and he had to close his eyes against the need to pick her up and carry her back to his bed.

"When I woke up, you weren't there. I wondered where you were." Her warm breath through his shirt felt as if she'd branded him as hers.

Digging deep for the strength to do what he knew was best for both of them, he said, "Abby, we have to talk."

She tightened her hold on him. "This sounds serious."

Taking her hands in his, he removed her arms from around him and turned to face her. He caught his breath.

She had never looked more beautiful than she did now, wearing nothing but his tuxedo shirt.

"Russ?"

"I've been thinking and…" He stopped to clear his throat, then rushed on before he could change his mind, grab her with both arms and hang on for dear life. "I don't think we should see each other anymore, Abby."

The hurt he saw in her expressive green eyes just about ripped his heart right out of his chest, but he admired the way she met his gaze head-on. "Could I ask what brought you to this conclusion?"

He shrugged. "A combination of a lot of things."

"Would you care to enlighten me?" Her voice shook slightly, and it just about tore him apart.

He should have known she'd want an in-depth explanation. "You really haven't figured it out by now?"

"I wouldn't be asking if I had," she said, wrapping her arms around her middle.

His hand was less than steady when he rubbed the tension building at the back of his neck. He hated having to call attention to all the ways he came up lacking. But if that's what it took to make her see reason, then that's what he'd do.

"Think about it, Abby. I don't have a damned thing to offer you, or any other woman." He shook his head. "Hell, I don't even own my own place."

"And you think that matters to me?" she asked incredulously. "If that's all you're basing your opinion on—"

"No, damn it, it's not. Don't you understand? I'm not good enough for you." It looked like he was going to have to spell it out for her. "You're a doctor of veterinary medicine, for God's sake. What could you possibly see in a man with nothing more than a high-school education?"

"I see a man who is kind, considerate and cares deeply about others," she said softly. "And you're an absolute genius when it comes to growing things."

Russ felt like he was getting nowhere fast, and the longer it took to convince her they could never make a go of it together, the bigger the chance his resolve would weaken. He hated himself for what he was about to say. It was a total lie, and he'd rather tear out his own heart than have to say the words that he knew would crush her emotionally. But it looked like he didn't have a choice.

"I thought you knew from the beginning that I was just showing you a good time while you were visiting The Vines. I didn't realize that you thought things were getting serious between us." He took a deep breath in order to force the lie past his tightening throat. "It's been fun, but it's time for both of us to move on."

She recoiled as if he'd struck her, and the horrified look on her face caused the knot twisting his gut to clench painfully. But as he watched, she raised her chin a notch and squared her slender shoulders.

"I'm sorry I misunderstood the situation," she said, her voice flat and emotionless. "I'll be out of your way as soon as I get dressed."

Without another word, she turned, and Russ watched her walk proudly toward his bedroom. Even though she had to be hurting as much as he was, she wasn't about to let him see her break down. It just wasn't her style. She had more courage and class than that.

Feeling like the biggest jerk who ever walked on two legs, he waited until she walked back into the living area. "I'll drive you to the carriage house."

"That won't be necessary," she said, shaking her head. "I know the way."

"Yes, but—"

"I'll be fine, Russ. You said yourself that it's over between us, and that includes you taking me anywhere." The ring of finality in her words just about tore him apart.

When she reached for the doorknob, he had to clench his fists at his sides to keep from reaching for her. "Goodbye, Abby."

He wasn't surprised when she didn't answer him and simply stepped out onto the small porch and closed the door behind her. The quiet click as she pulled it shut sounded like a cannon going off in the ominously silent room. And for the first time since losing his folks in that car accident eleven years ago, Russ found himself fighting back a wave of emotion so strong, it all but knocked him to his knees.

"Why am I not surprised to find you here?"

When Russ looked up to find Lucas and Caroline's son, Mason, walking toward him down the center aisle of the stables, he smiled. "Probably because it's winter and I don't have a whole hell of a lot to do in the vineyard." Seeing each other for the first time in months, the two friends hugged like brothers. "How was France?"

Mason gave him a teasing grin. "The wine is so-so compared to what we make here at Louret, the food is good and the women…well, they're French."

Russ chuckled. "And you've sampled your share of all three."

"Oh, yeah." Mason laughed. "Wouldn't you?"

"Probably," Russ said, noncommittally. Being with any woman other than Abby held about as much appeal to him as having a root canal.

"Whoa! Back up there, buddy." Mason's blue eyes twinkled with mischief. "What's happened while I was gone? Did some woman take you off the market?"

"No."

Mason's easy expression faded into a look of concern. "What's going on, Russ?"

"Nothing." He should have known his best friend would pick up on his pensive mood. Forcing a smile, Russ added, "Things are about the same as always. I'm working in the vineyards during the week and riding bulls on the weekends. In fact, I'm getting ready to leave this afternoon for a rodeo in Pine Creek."

"I'm not buying that it's the same old, same old," Mason said, shaking his head. "You might be able to fool somebody else, but I know you better than that." He placed his hand on Russ's shoulder. "You still keep a beer or two in the refrigerator in the tack room?"

"You know I do." Russ had a sinking feeling that Mason wasn't going to let the matter rest.

"Come on," the man said, motioning for Russ to follow him. "Let's down a cold one while you tell me what's put you into a tailspin."

Seeing no other alternative, Russ walked into the tack room and removed two aluminum cans from the refrigerator. He handed one to Mason, then popped the tab on the other and sat down beside his friend on the wooden bench by the supply cabinet. "There really isn't a lot to tell. I met a woman. We shared a few good times, but now it's over. End of story."

"I don't think so." Mason took a swig of his beer, then shook his blond head. "I know it's none of my business, but you look too damned miserable for that to be all there is to the story."

"It won't matter in another few days, anyway," Russ said, shrugging. He tipped the can and took a swallow of beer. "The lady in question will be leaving Napa soon."

The can he held was halfway to his mouth when Mason stopped to stare at him. "Well, I'll be damned. You're talking about Abigail Ashton, aren't you?" When Russ remained silent, his friend nodded. "I should have known. You've always had a thing for redheads, and she's a real knockout."

"You've met her?"

Mason nodded. "I stopped by the winery before I came down here to the stables. She was in the office and Mercedes introduced us."

Knowing that his friend wasn't going to give up until he had the whole story, Russ blew out a frustrated breath and told him about Abby and how amazing she was. "But I ended things with her yesterday."

"Why?"

"Because she deserves better than what I can give her," Russ answered truthfully.

Mason uttered an expletive that would have had Caroline washing his mouth out with a bar of soap if she'd heard it. "Where the hell is your head, Gannon? Don't you think you should have left that decision up to her?"

"One of us had to be practical." Russ downed the rest

of his beer. "Let's face it, a woman like Abby couldn't be happy for the rest of her life with a guy like me."

"Okay, now I know you're sitting on your brains," Mason said, sounding disgusted.

Russ crushed his beer can with his hand, then tossed it in the trash. "Name me one well-educated woman you know who's found lasting happiness with a blue-collar man with nothing more going for him than the ability to grow a few grapes."

"How about my mother?" Mason looked smug. "She and my dad have been head over heels in love with each other for the past twenty-seven years. I'd say that qualifies as a prime example of lasting happiness." Rising to his feet, Mason tossed his beer can, then picked up one of the saddles. "Chew on that little bit of food for thought as you drive down to Pine Creek. You can let me know I'm right when you get back."

"Did anyone ever tell you that you're a smart-ass, Sheppard?" Russ grumbled.

Mason laughed. "Yeah. You tell me every time you know I'm right about something."

Abby bit her lower lip to keep it from trembling as she hung the green silk dress she'd worn to the Ashton estate in her garment bag, then turned to finish packing her suitcase. She was glad she'd gotten acquainted with her California relatives, but the time had come for her to go back to Nebraska.

Feeling utterly defeated, she sat on the side of the bed and stared at the brochure from the Wild Horse Flats rodeo she'd attended with Russ. She had no idea why she'd kept it. Normally, she wasn't sentimental about those kinds of things. But as she stared at the colorful paper advertising the different events, a fresh wave of emotion swept over her.

Why was he doing this to them?

She hadn't for a second bought into that line of hooey he'd tried to feed her yesterday morning when he'd told her it's been fun, but now it's over. He was too considerate, too caring, to ever take what they'd shared that lightly. In fact, he'd told her before they ever made love that he'd walk away from their relationship before he did anything that would hurt her.

The air suddenly lodged in her lungs and her heart began to thump a wild tattoo. He'd said that he had nothing to offer a woman. He'd told her that he didn't even own a home. And he'd mentioned the differences in their educations. But she'd been so stunned and hurt that she'd only focused on the fact that he was rejecting her, not on what he'd really been trying to tell her. The poor, misguided man couldn't be more wrong.

"My God, he's making us both miserable because he thinks he's doing what's best for me," she said aloud.

She bit her lip as she tried to think of what to do. For years, she'd been afraid of turning out like her mother.

But Grace had never been satisfied and always thought she deserved better than the simple lifestyle a man of the land could provide. And that was all Abby had ever wanted.

But how was she ever going to convince Russ of that?

Before she had the chance to review her options and decide what she could do, there was a light tap on the door frame. Looking up, Abby found Mercedes standing at the open door.

"Are you all right?"

Abby took a deep breath and nodded. "I'm going to be fine. However, one hardheaded vineyard foreman has reason to be extremely worried."

Mercedes frowned as she walked over to sit beside her on the bed. "Did I miss something? I thought you and Russ had parted ways and you were going back to Nebraska."

"I changed my mind." For the first time since she'd left the cottage yesterday morning, Abby smiled. "I'm not going anywhere until he's listened to what I have to say. He might be ready to give up on us, but I'm not."

"Oh, I definitely like the sound of this," Mercedes said, grinning.

Abby nibbled on her lower lip. "Now, if I could just remember where he told me he was competing this weekend."

"Leave that to me," Mercedes said, reaching for the phone. "When do you want to leave?"

"As soon as possible." Having waited twenty-four years to find the man of her dreams, Abby wasn't about to waste a minute longer than she had to.

As Russ stood in line to pay his entry fees and collect his back number for the bull-riding event, J. B. Gardner tapped him on the shoulder. "Is Abby in the stands with Nina?"

"No." A pang of regret that threatened to bend him double ran through Russ as he shook his head. "She didn't come with me this weekend."

"That's a shame," J.B. said, sounding disappointed. "Nina was really looking forward to talking to her."

Russ took a deep breath. "You can tell Nina not to count on that happening again."

"But I thought you two—"

"You thought wrong," Russ said, cutting off his friend. When the cowboy in front of him moved out of the way, he paid his fee to the official seated at the entry table and accepted the back number the man handed him. Turning back to J.B., he felt guilty for having been so curt. "Look, I'm sorry, but it's a sore subject right now."

J.B. nodded sympathetically. "She dump you?"

Shaking his head, Russ took a deep breath as he stepped aside for his friend to pay his entry. "I called a halt to it."

"Have you lost your mind?" J.B. asked. "It was clear as the nose on your face that girl was crazy about you."

"Thanks, J.B. You're really making me feel better," Russ said, unable to keep the sarcasm from his voice.

His friend placed an understanding hand on his shoulder. "Any chance of you two getting things worked out?"

Russ shook his head. "I doubt it."

Without waiting for J.B., Russ picked up his duffel bag and slowly walked to the dressing area where the cowboys stored their gear and got ready for their events. He should be concentrating on what he knew about the bull he'd drawn, stretching his muscles and preparing himself mentally for his upcoming ride. Instead, his mind was about a hundred miles away.

What was Abby doing now? Was she packing to leave The Vines? Or had she already caught a flight to go back home to Nebraska?

As he put on his chaps, he mulled over what Mason had said about a well-educated woman being able to find lasting happiness with a simple man like himself. It was true that Caroline and Lucas Sheppard had made a good life together, and anyone who knew them could verify the fact that they loved each other and were very happy. But could he and Abby do the same?

Buckling the last of the chaps' leather straps, Russ sank down onto one of the benches in the dressing room and thought about how much Abby meant to him. He'd never been in love before, but he knew beyond a shadow of doubt that he loved her with all of his heart and soul.

She'd said that his lack of a college education didn't matter to her, nor did she care that he didn't have much of anything to offer her beyond himself. But could she really be happy with him for the rest of their days? Had he made the biggest mistake of his life when he'd broken things off with her?

"Hey, Gannon, are you going to sit there daydreaming, or are you going to ride your draw?" one of the other bull riders called from the doorway. "You're up next."

Rising to his feet, he walked to the back of the bucking chutes and climbed the steps to the raised platform. He cringed when he noticed his draw. The Shredder had a wicked set of horns, and had earned his name because of the way he used them after he'd bucked off a rider.

When a cowboy tied himself to the back of a bull, he needed every ounce of concentration he possessed to make a successful ride. But The Shredder was bad news, even when a rider had his mind on the business at hand. Unfortunately, Russ wasn't concentrating on the bull he was about to ride. He was too busy thinking about the only woman he'd ever loved.

But taking a turn out wasn't his style, and, stepping over the side of the chute, he settled himself on the dun-colored Brahma's back. J.B. helped him pull his rope tight around the bull's belly, then handed the excess to Russ for him to wrap around his hand.

"You sure you want to do this?" J.B. asked, looking doubtful.

"I might as well," Russ answered, as he jammed his Resistol down tight on his head to keep from losing it during the ride. "In case you hadn't noticed, it's a little late to back out now."

"Then, cowboy, up and ride that son of a gun," J.B. said, grinning.

Russ knew what his friend was trying to do. J.B. was trying to pump him up and get Russ to concentrate on staying with the bull, jump for jump. He appreciated the encouragement, but as he slipped his mouth guard into place and nodded for the gate man to open the chute, he realized it was going to take more than J.B.'s good wishes for him to make a successful ride.

The Shredder came out of the chute as though someone had set off a keg of dynamite under him, and the first bone-jarring jump had Russ shifting his weight to stay in the middle of the big animal's back. But he knew he was in serious trouble when the bull twisted in midair, then settled into a flat spin. Jerked backward and to the side, centrifugal force took over, and Russ found himself flying through the air sideways. His landing on the soft dirt floor of the arena wasn't graceful, but as the bullfighters moved in, he thanked the good Lord above that nothing more than his pride had been damaged.

He started to scramble to his feet and sprint for the safety of the fence, but it suddenly felt as if he'd been hit from behind by a freight train. All of the air left his lungs in one big *whoosh,* and as he fell forward, he felt something hard connect with the side of his head. Pain exploded behind his eyes, and as the peaceful curtain of unconsciousness began to close in around him, his last thought and the last word on his lips was, "Abby."

Ten

By the time she and Nina had made their way from the seats to the training room at the back of the stadium, Abby was shaking all over, and her heart pounded inside her chest. She'd been horrified to see the big, ugly bull ignore the bullfighters and set his sights on running Russ down. But when one of the animal's hooves grazed his head, knocking him unconscious, she'd thought she'd die right then and there. She'd never in her life experienced such abject terror.

"I'm sorry, ladies, but you'll have to return to your seats," a security guard said, stopping them in the hall.

"The only people allowed in the training room are medical personnel."

Thinking fast, Abby nodded. "My name is Dr. Abigail Ashton. I'm Mr. Gannon's doctor."

Technically, she did have a medical degree, just not one for treating people. That's why she'd purposely avoided calling herself Russ's "physician." But the guard didn't know she was a veterinarian, and she wasn't about to enlighten him. All that mattered was her getting to Russ.

The man looked uncertain. "Do you have some kind of identification?"

"Sure, doesn't every doctor carry their degree around with them?" Abby asked sarcastically. But she pulled her wallet from her purse and showed him her driver's license and a credit card issued to Dr. Abigail Ashton. Fortunately, the company that had sent her the card had failed to include the initials *DVM* after her name. "Now, get out of my way or I swear you'll be standing in the unemployment line Monday morning."

"Yes, ma'am," he said, stepping aside.

As they hurried on down the hall, Nina stared at her wide-eyed. "I didn't know you're a doctor."

"I'm not." Abby shrugged. "At least, not a medical doctor. I'm a large-animal vet."

Nina grinned. "Whatever. It worked to get you in to see Russ."

"It was going to take a lot more than one middle-aged

security guard to keep me out," Abby said, meaning it. When she saw J.B. standing outside of a door at the far end of the hall, she asked, "How is he?"

"Out like a light. But don't worry," he hurried to add. "The doc said Russ should be coming around any time."

"Are there any internal injuries?"

J.B. shook his head as he put his arm around Nina. "Russ was wearing his riding vest. It saved him from being hooked by the bull's horns."

"Thanks for the update," Abby said, breathing a sigh of relief as she entered the training room.

A man wearing a black-and-white striped vest, designating him as one of the medical personnel, smiled when she walked up to the side of the gurney where Russ lay. "Are you with Gannon?"

She nodded. "Has he regained consciousness yet?"

"He's in and out," the man said, pulling a chair over beside the stretcher. At her questioning look, he shrugged. "You might want to sit a spell."

As she stood looking down at the man she loved more than life itself, her chest tightened. Russ had a bruise on his left cheek and a lump the size of a goose egg on the side of his head, but otherwise he didn't look bad.

Taking his hand in hers, she felt his fingers move slightly. "Russ, darling, wake up," she said softly.

He murmured her name, and his hand tightened around hers a moment before his eyelids slowly opened and he fixed his blue gaze on her. "A-Abby?"

She brushed his dark blond hair away from his forehead as she looked for any other signs of injury. "I'm right here, Russ."

"You can't be," he said, sounding tired. He closed his eyes, and his jaw muscles clenched as if he were in pain. "You're on your way back to Nebraska."

She placed her hand on his brow and leaned down to lightly kiss his firm lips. "No, darling. I'm right here with you. Where I belong."

His eyes snapped open, and this time she could tell he was fully conscious. "I'm not hallucinating?"

Turning to the emergency medical technician, she asked, "Could you give us a moment alone?"

Nodding, the man silently left the room.

"No, Russ, you're not hallucinating."

"But I—"

"You can't get rid of me that easily." She released his hand and sat down in the chair. "You might be ready to give up on us, but I'm not."

"You're not?"

The look of relief crossing his handsome face was all the encouragement she needed to continue. "Not by a long shot, cowboy. I listened to you yesterday morning, now you're going to hear what I have to say."

"I am?" He gave her a lopsided grin, and she wondered if he might not be too groggy to listen to her.

But taking a deep breath, she met his amused gaze head-on. "I'm not willing to give you up without a fight."

He ran his index finger along her cheek. "I don't think I'm in much shape for a fight, honey."

"Good." His touch felt like heaven and she had to remind herself that she had something more she needed to say. "Before you hear what I drove over two hours to tell you, I have a question."

"What's that?" His deep baritone sent a shiver of need straight to her core.

Abby did her best to ignore the sensation and pressed on. "Where on God's green earth did you get the idea that you weren't good enough for me?"

He frowned, then winced and reached up to rub the side of his head. Apparently, the facial movement had caused the lump just above his temple to hurt.

"I don't have the education—"

"That's a bunch of bull and we both know it." At his startled expression, she smiled. "We all have our place in life, and you have a gift that I've always wanted, but will never have. You can grow just about anything, anywhere your heart desires."

He shrugged one shoulder. "Anyone can do it."

She shook her head. "No, they can't. Do you want to

know the reason I went into veterinary medicine, instead of agriculture?"

"Because you like animals?"

"That's the main reason," she said nodding. "But the other reason is because I kill everything I try to grow. I can't even keep a houseplant alive. Whenever I bring one home, Uncle Grant and Ford make jokes about another innocent plant being doomed to an untimely and torturous end."

"You're probably just trying too hard," he said, chuckling.

"I don't think so." She took hold of his hands. "Don't you see, Russ? Your talent is right here in the calluses you have from making things grow. You may not have a college degree, but that doesn't make you any less of an expert at what you do."

He looked thoughtful and she could tell he was digesting what she'd told him. "I've never looked at it that way," he finally said. "But you might have a point."

"Well, it's about time you came to that conclusion." When he acted as if he was going to get up, she stood up and gently pushed him back down on the stretcher. "I'm not finished talking."

He grinned. "Did anyone ever tell you that you're a bossy little number?"

"I think I've heard that before." She laughed as she remembered what they'd said to each other that first day in the stable. "Did anyone ever tell you that you're slower than molasses in January?"

Chuckling, he reached up to pull her down to him. "Come here, honey."

Abby shook her head. "I told you, I have more to say." When he started to protest, she placed her index finger to his lips. "I love you with all my heart, Russ Gannon."

"You love me?" His sexy grin caused her stomach to flutter.

"Yes, I do. But I have something I need to confess."

He suddenly looked a bit wary. "What's that?"

"Do you know why I remained a virgin while most girls my age have been sexually active for years?"

"You were worried you'd turn out like your mother."

"That's true," she admitted. "But that's not the entire reason."

His smile was understanding when he nodded. "You were afraid most guys would be like old Harold and not take 'no' for an answer."

"Not even close." Smiling at his surprised expression, she cupped his lean cheek with her palm. "Russ, I waited to give myself to the man I wanted to spend the rest of my life with. And whether you like it or not, you're that man."

His grin was back full force. "Is that a marriage proposal?"

"Call it what you will, it's the truth. You're all the man I'll ever want or need," she said softly.

"God, Abby, I love you more than life itself," he said, sitting up to pull her to him. "If you'll have me, I'll spend the rest of my life proving it to you."

"I'm going to hold you to that, cowboy," she said, kissing him until they both gasped for breath. Grinning, she added, "Oh, there's one more thing that you probably need to know."

"What's that, honey?"

"After we get married, there won't be an issue of you not owning your own place." At his questioning look, she smiled. "A third of that big Nebraska farm is mine, and once I'm Mrs. Russ Gannon, it will be yours, too."

He shook his head. "I don't want your land. All I want is you. We'll move to Nebraska and I'll help work the farm, but we'll have a prenuptial agreement drawn up—"

"No, we won't." She kissed him again. "We'll be in this marriage together. Forever. What's mine will be yours and what's yours, will be mine. You got that straight, cowboy?"

He laughed. "Yeah, I think I've finally got it." His expression turned serious. "I love you, Abby."

"And I love you, Russ. With all of my heart."

A week later, Abby glanced at her checklist. The cake would be delivered tomorrow morning and so would the flowers. She and Russ had their marriage license and their rings. But it felt like she was forgetting something.

"Oh, dear God, I forgot to pick Ford up at the airport."

Grabbing the keys to the car she'd rented, she rushed down the carriage house stairs. How could she have forgotten to pick up her brother?

"Where's the fire, sis?" a familiar voice asked as she hurried toward the door.

When she spun around, she saw Ford and Uncle Grant sitting at the kitchen table, looking thoroughly amused. "How did you get here? I mean, when did you get here?" She shook her head. "Oh, I don't care. I'm just glad you're here."

"Uncle Grant. About an hour ago. And I'm glad to see you, too," Ford said, rising to his feet to give her a bear hug. "How's the bride?"

"Scared spitless that I'll forget something," she said, wondering if she should go check her list again. If she hadn't remembered something as important as meeting her brother at the airport, what else had she missed?

"Relax, Sprite," Uncle Grant said, smiling. "Everything will work out."

"Did you pick up your tux?" She thought he'd told her he had, but she decided double-checking wasn't a bad idea, all things considered.

Laughing, her uncle nodded. "And I got the haircut you told me I needed."

With his arm around her shoulders, Ford smiled. "Abby?"

"What?"

"Breathe."

She sighed. "I'm not sure I have time."

Uncle Grant smiled. "Everything is under control, Sprite. Caroline and Mercedes have the ceremony and reception covered, and there really isn't anything left to do but walk down the aisle tomorrow." He rose to his feet and placed his coffee cup in the sink. "Why don't you take a break from all this wedding stuff and introduce Ford to his brother-in-law-to-be?"

Ford nodded. "Yeah. I have a few things I want to discuss with this guy."

"Oh, stop the overprotective-big-brother act," Abby said, grinning. "You're going to love Russ."

"I doubt that." Ford shook his head emphatically. "I don't love guys."

Happy for the excuse to see Russ before the wedding rehearsal that night, she removed her jacket from the coat tree beside the door, then took Ford by the arm to pull him along. "Stop your macho act and come on. I can't wait for you to meet Russ."

As they walked toward the stable, Ford asked, "What's going on with Uncle Grant?"

Abby had expected Ford to question her on what their uncle had been doing in Napa Valley. When she'd called to ask him to come to California for her wedding, Ford had expressed his concern about their uncle's obsession with meeting Spencer Ashton.

"He says he's going to stay as long as it takes to see Spencer," she answered.

"On the ride from the airport he said he's going to the media with the story about Spencer's illegal marriage to Caroline," Ford said. "He's hoping that gets the bastard's attention."

"Nothing else has worked." Her heart ached for Uncle Grant. He was such a good man. He deserved answers to his questions about why his father walked away all those years ago. "I don't think Uncle Grant wanted it to come to this, but Spencer didn't give him any other choice."

Ford nodded. "At least one good thing has come from this mess."

"And that would be?" she asked as they entered the stable.

"We're getting you married off."

Abby laughed. "Yes, but I'm not leaving home. Russ and I are going to live on the farm."

"Did I hear my name mentioned?" Russ asked, stepping out of the tack room. He walked up to her, wrapped his arms around her and kissed her until she felt lightheaded. "How's my best girl?"

"She'd better be your only girl," Ford said firmly.

Russ nodded. "The one and only. Unless, of course, we have a daughter."

Ford's eyes narrowed. "Abby are you—"

"No."

Russ figured he'd be talking to Abby's brother at some point before the wedding. He'd already received a fatherly speech from her uncle.

"Honey, as much as I'd like to spend the rest of the day holding you, I think Mercedes was looking for you earlier. Why don't you go up to the winery and see if she needs your help with something?" He gave Ford a meaningful look. "I'll keep your brother company while you're gone."

"That sounds like a good idea," Ford said, nodding.

"You're not fooling me." She rolled her eyes and shook her head. "Ford is going to give you the brotherly warning. And you're going to tell him that he has nothing to worry about." She gave him a quick kiss. "Just remember, I don't want any black eyes or split lips in my wedding photos."

Both Russ and Ford remained silent while they watched her walk out of the stable and down the path toward the winery.

"You're going to have your hands full," Ford warned. "There isn't a whole lot that gets past her."

Grinning, Russ nodded. "I wouldn't want her to be any other way." He motioned for Ford to follow him. "How would you like to give me the brotherly lecture over a beer?"

"Gannon, I have a feeling you and I are going to get along just fine," Ford said, grinning.

The next afternoon, in the upstairs bedroom Mercedes said had been hers when she still lived at The Vines, Abby stared at herself in the full-length mirror. The dress she and Mercedes had picked out truly was gorgeous. With a scoop neckline and tiny seed pearls adorning the white lace and satin, it made her feel like a princess.

"You look beautiful, Abby," Caroline said, adjusting her veil.

"Is Russ here?"

"Yes, dear." Caroline gave her an indulgent smile. "In fact, I think he arrived an hour earlier than the time Mercedes told him to be here."

Turning to face her, Abby smiled at the woman who had been kind enough to offer her home for the wedding. Caroline had even insisted on helping pull the wedding together on short notice in order for Abby to return home and start her clinic in time for the calving season. "Thank you, Caroline. I truly appreciate everything you've done for my family."

"Lucas and I have been happy to have you here at The Vines," Caroline said, her smile genuine. "You, Grant and Ford are part of our family now."

Tears blurring her vision, Abby hugged the older woman. "You're the best."

Caroline embraced her, then, stepping back, dabbed at her eyes with a lace handkerchief. "Russ is like a son to us, and I couldn't be happier for both of you."

A tap on the door drew their attention a moment before Uncle Grant stepped into the room. Tall, with just a touch of gray at his temples, he looked very distinguished and handsome in his black tuxedo.

"My God, Sprite, you're beautiful."

"You're not so bad yourself," she said, walking into his open arms.

"I can't believe you're old enough to be getting married," he said gruffly as he held her close. "It seems like just yesterday I was bandaging your scraped knees and helping you with your homework."

"It's time," Mercedes said, entering the room in a rush. "And it's a good thing, too." She laughed. "Mason and Ford have already threatened to tie Russ down if he doesn't stop pacing."

"I'll see you downstairs, dear," Caroline said, lightly kissing Abby's cheek.

Mercedes sniffed back tears as she handed Abby a bouquet of pink roses and white baby's breath, then, giving her a quick hug, followed Caroline from the room.

"Are you ready to give me away?" Abby asked when she and her uncle stood at the top of the stairs.

"I'll walk you downstairs and I'll place your hand in Russ's." He shook his head as he offered her his arm.

"But I'm not giving you away. You'll always be my little Sprite. I want you to remember that, Abby."

Tears filled her eyes. "I love you, Uncle Grant. Thank you for taking care of me and Ford all these years."

"I wouldn't have had it any other way, Sprite," he said, placing his hand over hers where it rested in the crook of his arm.

As much as she loved her uncle, when they descended the circular staircase and she caught sight of Russ standing by the fireplace in the living room, Abby forgot everything else and focused on the man she loved. He looked so handsome that her heart skipped several beats.

Stopping in front of him, Uncle Grant placed her hand in Russ's. "Love her and take care of her."

"For the rest of my life," Russ said, his gaze never leaving hers.

"I love you, Russ."

"And I love you, honey."

Uncle Grant gave them both a fatherly smile, then, kissing her cheek, stepped aside. And Abby pledged herself to the only man she knew she'd ever love.

* * * * *

The scandals and sensuality continue!
Megan Ashton hadn't planned on getting married quite
so soon, and certainly not to a stranger! But when
charming playboy Simon Pearce had asked her to be his
stand-in bride, he offered her a deal she couldn't refuse.
Theirs was purely a business arrangement—as long as
both of them could keep their emotions in check, and
their thoughts out of the bedroom….

Don't miss SOCIETY-PAGE SEDUCTION
by Maureen Child, the third book in
Silhouette Desire's in-line continuity:
DYNASTIES: THE ASHTONS
Available March 2005

Silhouette
Desire®

Are you a ♥ chocolate lover?

Try WALDORF CHOCOLATE FONDUE— a true chocolate decadence

While many couples choose to dine out on Valentine's Day, one of the most romantic things you can do for your sweetheart is to prepare an elegant meal—right in the comfort of your own home.

Harlequin asked John Doherty, executive chef at the Waldorf-Astoria Hotel in New York City, for his recipe for seduction—the famous Waldorf Chocolate Fondue....

WALDORF CHOCOLATE FONDUE
Serves 6-8

2 cups water
½ cup corn syrup
1 cup sugar
8 oz dark bitter chocolate, chopped
1 pound cake (can be purchased in supermarket)
2–3 cups assorted berries
2 cups pineapple
½ cup peanut brittle

Bring water, corn syrup and sugar to a boil in a medium-size pot. Turn off the heat and add the chopped chocolate. Strain and pour into fondue pot. Cut cake and fruit into cubes and 1-inch pieces. Place fondue pot in the center of a serving plate, arrange cake, fruit and peanut brittle around pot. Serve with forks.

An Invitation for Love

hot
tips

Find a special way to invite your guy into your
Harlequin Moment. Letting him know you're
looking for a little romance will help put his
mind on the same page as yours. In fact,
if you do it right, he won't be able to stop
thinking about you until he sees you again!

Send him a long-stemmed rose tied to an invitation
that leaves a lot up to the imagination.

Autograph a favorite photo of you and tape it on
the appointed day in his day planner. Block out
the hours he'll be spending with you.

Send him a local map and put an *X* on the place you
want him to meet you. Write: "I'm lost without you.
Come find me. Tonight at 8." Use magazine cutouts
and photographs to paste images of romance and
the two of you all over the map.

Send him something personal that he'll recognize as
yours to his office. Write: "If found, please return.
Owner offers reward to anyone returning item by
7:30 on Saturday night." Don't sign the card.

COMING NEXT MONTH

SDCNM0205